"I want to make love to you."

Her mouth fell open. *"Marcus!"*

He shook his head. "You should never have come back if you didn't want this to happen," he told her softly. "Nine years ago we blew everything—and I want the chance to put it right."

"Oh. I see. Was I the one lover who didn't give you full marks for performance? Is that what this is all about?"

"No. It's about getting rid of a desire that isn't going to go away. Look me in the eye, Donna, and tell me truthfully that you don't want me just as badly. Do that and I'll go away and leave you alone."

She couldn't.

He whispered, "Give in to what you really want to do. Kiss me."

Sharon Kendrick

HER SECRET PREGNANCY

TORONTO • NEW YORK • LONDON
AMSTERDAM • PARIS • SYDNEY • HAMBURG
STOCKHOLM • ATHENS • TOKYO • MILAN • MADRID
PRAGUE • WARSAW • BUDAPEST • AUCKLAND

To Judy and Rob Hutson
with thanks for their vision and imagination.

ISBN 0-373-12198-9

HER SECRET PREGNANCY

First North American Publication 2001.

Copyright © 2000 by Sharon Kendrick.

Visit us at www.eHarlequin.com

Printed in U.S.A.

CHAPTER ONE

THE lawyer was slick and smooth and handsome—with the most immaculately manicured hands that Donna had ever seen.

'Okay, Donna, if you'd like to sign just there.' He jabbed a near-perfect fingernail onto the contract. 'See? Right there.'

Donna was tempted to giggle. 'You mean where your secretary has helpfully drawn a little cross?'

'Ah, yes. Sorry,' he amended quickly. 'I didn't mean to patronise you.'

The tension of the last few weeks dissolved. 'Don't worry. You weren't.' She signed her name with a flourish. 'I'm just glad it's all over.'

Tony Paxman did not look as though he echoed her sentiments. 'I shall miss seeing you!' he sighed. 'Still, the premises are yours and you've got your liquour licence. Now it's over to you. Congratulations, Donna!' He held his hand out. 'And I wish you every success for the future!'

'Thank you,' said Donna, hoping she didn't sound smug. Or triumphant. Because she knew she should be neither. She was just lucky—though some people said there was no such thing, that you made your own luck in life.

She picked up her cream silk jacket and gave Tony Paxman a grateful smile. He had guided her through all the paperwork concerning the purchase with the care of a soldier negotiating a treacherous minefield. Most importantly of all, he'd kept the whole deal quiet. She owed him. 'Would you like to have lunch with me, to celebrate?'

Tony blinked with the kind of surprise which suggested that a lunch invitation from Donna King had been the very last thing in the world he had been expecting. 'Lunch?' he said weakly.

Donna raised her eyebrows at him. She wasn't proposing an illicit weekend in Paris! 'Or have I broken some kind of unwritten law by inviting you?'

He shook his head hastily. 'Oh, no, no, no! I often have lunch with my clients—'

'That's what I thought.' She glanced down at her watch. 'Shall we say one o'clock? In The New Hampshire?'

'The New Hampshire?' Tony Paxman gave a regretful smile. 'Marcus Foreman's place? I'd absolutely love to—but we won't get a table today. Not at such short notice, I'm afraid. Not a chance in hell.'

'I know that.' Donna smiled. 'Which is why I took the precaution of making a reservation weeks ago.'

He frowned. 'You were so sure we'd wrap up the deal?'

'Pretty much. I knew that the court hearing to get my licence was today. And I didn't foresee any problems.'

'You know, you're a very confident woman, Donna King,' he told her softly. 'As well as being an extremely beautiful one.'

Time to gently destroy his embryo fantasies. It was just a pity that some men saw a simple gesture of friendship as an invitation to form some deep and meaningful relationship.

'Please don't get the wrong idea, Tony,' she told him softly. 'This is purely a business lunch—a way of me thanking you for all your hard work. That's all. Nothing more.'

'Right.' He began to move papers around on his desk with a sudden urgency. 'Then I'll see you in The New Hampshire at one o'clock, shall I?'

'Yes, indeed,' said Donna. She reached for her bag and rose to her feet, the high heels of her brown suede shoes making her look much taller than usual. 'I shall look forward to it.'

'Me, too,' he said wistfully.

Outside the lawyer's office, Donna sucked in the crisp April air, scarcely able to believe she was back in the city she loved. Her visits over the last few weeks had been secretive, but there was no need for secrecy any longer. She was here—and here to stay.

It was a perfect day. Blue sky. Golden sun. The white waxy petals of a magnolia shining out like stars. A grey stone church whose spire looked like the sharpened tip of a pencil. Perfect. And the cherry on top of the cake was that she had swung the deal.

People had said that she was crazy to open up a tea-room in a city like Winchester, which was already bursting to the seams with places to eat. And they'd had a point. But most of those places were indifferent, and most were owned by large, faceless chains. Only one stood out from the crowd. And it belonged to Marcus Foreman.

Donna swallowed down excitement and nerves and something else, too. Something she hadn't felt in so long she had thought she'd never feel it again. A lost, forgotten feeling. But it was there, potent and tugging and insistent just at the thought that very soon she would see Marcus again. Excitement.

And not the kind of excitement you got the night before you went on holiday, either. This was the kind that made the tips of your breasts prickle and your limbs grow weak.

'Oh, damn!' she said aloud. 'Damn and damn and damn!' And, turning her collar up against the sudden, sharp reminder that the breeze which blew in springtime had an icy bite to it, Donna set off down the street to window-shop until lunchtime.

She walked slowly around the shops, only half seeing the clothes in the expensive boutiques which studded the city like diamonds in an eternity band. Exquisite clothes in natural fibres of silk and cotton and cashmere. Clothes which would normally tempt her into looking, even if she couldn't always afford to buy.

But today was not a normal day. And not just because it wasn't every day that you ploughed your savings into buying a business which several people had predicted would fail from the start.

No, today was different, because as well as going for-ward—Donna would be going back. Back to the place where she'd met Marcus and learned about love and loss—and a whole lot more besides.

It was just past one when she sauntered her way into the reception area of The New Hampshire, hoping that she looked more confident than she felt. Behind the smooth, pale mask of her carefully made-up face, she could feel the unfamiliar thumping of nerves as she looked around her.

The place had changed out of all recognition. When Donna had worked there it had been during the chintz era, when everything had been tucked and swagged and covered with tiny sprigs of flowers.

But Marcus had clearly moved with the times. The carpet had disappeared and so had the chintz. Now there were bare, beautifully polished wood floorboards and simple curtains at the vast windows. The furniture had been kept to a minimum, and it looked simple and comfortable rather than in-your-face opulent. Definitely no overstuffed sofas!

Donna remembered how overwhelmed she'd felt the very first time she'd walked in through those doors. It had been like entering another world. But she'd been just eighteen then—nine years and a lifetime ago.

She walked up to the reception desk on which sat a giant glass bowl containing scented flowers. The fleshy white lips of the lilies were gaping open, surrounded by spiky green foliage which looked like swords. It was an exquisite and sexy arrangement, but then Marcus had always had exquisite taste.

The receptionist looked up. 'Can I help you, madam?'

'Yes, hello—I have a table booked for lunch,' smiled Donna.

'Your name, please?'

'It's King. Donna King.' Her voice sounded unnaturally loud, and she half expected Marcus to jump out of the shadows to bar her way. 'And I'm meeting a Mr Tony Paxman.'

The receptionist was running her eyes down a list, and ticked off Donna's name before she looked up again.

'Ah, yes. Mr Paxman has already arrived.' She gave Donna a look of polite enquiry. 'Have you ever eaten at The New Hampshire before?'

Donna shook her head. 'No.'

She'd made beds and cleaned out baths and sinks in the rooms upstairs, and had worked her way through some of the more delicious leftovers which had found their way back to the kitchen. And just once she'd eaten with the rest of the staff in the private function room upstairs, when Marcus had been jubilantly celebrating a glowing newspaper review.

Donna swallowed down that particular memory. But she'd certainly never eaten a full meal in the fabulous restaurant.

'No, I haven't.'

'Then I'll get someone to show you to your table.'

Donna followed one of the waiters, determined not to feel intimidated, telling herself that she'd worked and eaten in places just like this all over the world.

Yet her heart was still racing with anticipation that she might see him, and she wondered why.

Because she was over Marcus.

She had been for years.

The restaurant was already almost full and Tony Paxman rose to his feet as she approached. 'I was beginning to think you'd stood me up!'

'Oh, ye of little faith!' she joked, smiling up at the waiter, who was hovering attentively. 'Some house champagne, please. We're celebrating!'

'Certainly, madam.'

Tony Paxman waited until he was on his second glass before remarking obscurely, 'Let's hope you'll still have something to celebrate six months down the line.'

The bubbles inside her mouth burst. 'Meaning?'

He shrugged. 'Just that Marcus Foreman won't exactly be overjoyed when he finds out that you're opening up a new restaurant in the same town.'

'Oh?' Donna slid a green olive into her mouth and chewed on it thoughtfully. 'Everyone knows he has an awesome reputation in the catering industry—surely he's man enough to take a little honest competition?'

'I should imagine he's man enough for most things,'

remarked Tony Paxman drily. 'Just maybe not in the very same street.'

Donna placed the olive stone in a small dish in front of her. 'Anyway, I'm hardly going to be a *serious* rival, am I? Think about it—his hotel only serves afternoon tea to its residents.'

'True. But what if they start coming to you instead?'

Donna shrugged. 'It's a free country, and there is always room for excellence.' She gave a huge smile as she lifted her glass in a toast. 'So may the best man win!'

'Or woman?' Tony murmured.

Donna looked down the menu, spoilt for choice. 'Let's order, shall we? I'm starving!'

'Sounds good. Then you can tell me your life story.' He frowned. 'You know, your hair is the most amazing golden-red colour. I bet you used to dress up as a princess when you were a little girl!'

'No, I was the one with the long face, wearing rags!' Donna joked, though it wasn't really a joke at all.

She'd experienced just about every emotion it was possible to feel about her itinerant childhood with a loving but ultimately foolish mother. At her knee she had learnt the arts of exaggeration and evasion, and had then learnt that they were just different words for lying. And lies could grow bigger and bigger, until they swamped you like a wave and dragged you under with them.

She smiled at Tony Paxman. 'Let's talk about you instead. And then you can tell me all about Winchester.'

He began to talk, and Donna tried very hard to enjoy the meal and his company. To make witty small-talk as adults always did. Pleasant chatter that didn't mean a thing.

But she was too distracted by her surroundings to be able to concentrate very much. Even on the food. Weird.

She hadn't banked on Marcus still being able to affect her desire to eat.

He'd always employed the most talented chefs—even in the early days, when he hadn't been able to afford to pay them very much. And it seemed that his standards hadn't slipped. Not by a fraction. Donna gazed at a perfect pyramid of chocolate mousse which sat in a puddle of banana sauce.

Maybe she *was* completely mad to set herself up in some sort of competition with a man who had always been regarded within the industry as having both flair and foresight.

'Donna,' said Tony suddenly.

She pushed the pudding plate away from her and looked up. 'Mmm?'

'Why did you ask me to have lunch with you today?' He swallowed a mouthful of wine and refilled his glass, then began answering his own question without appearing to notice he was doing it. 'Because it sure as hell wasn't because you wanted to take our relationship any further.'

She stared at him in confusion. 'But I told you that back in the office.'

'I guess you did.' He shrugged. 'Maybe I hoped I could change your mind.'

'Sorry,' she said softly, and sat back in her chair to look at him. 'The lunch is to say thank you.'

'For?'

'For tying up the deal without complications and for keeping it secret.'

'Ah, yes.' He sipped his drink and watched her. 'I meant to ask you about that. Why the big secret? Why wasn't anyone allowed to know?'

'It's no secret any more.' She smiled. 'You can tell who you like.'

He leaned across the table. 'You told me that you'd never eaten here before.'

'Well, I haven't.'

'But this isn't the first time you've been here, is it?'

Donna's eyes narrowed with interest. She hadn't been expecting perception. Not from him. 'What makes you say that?'

'Your body language. I spend my life observing it—goes with the job. I'm an expert!' he boasted.

Not such an expert, Donna thought, that he had been able to recognise that she was sending out don't-come-close messages. Still, there was no point trying to exist with misunderstanding and deceit flying around the place. She knew that more than anyone. 'I used to work here,' she told him. 'Years ago. When I was young.'

'You're hardly ancient now.'

'I'm twenty-seven!'

'Old enough to know better?' he teased.

'Oh, I don't think so,' came a silky drawl from behind Donna's right shoulder. 'Not if past experience is anything to go on. Don't you agree, Donna?'

She didn't turn around. She didn't need to. She would have recognised that voice if it had come distorted at her in the dark from a hundred miles away. A split-second of dazed recognition stretched out in front of her like a tightrope. She moved her head back by a fraction—and she could almost *feel* his presence, though she still couldn't see him.

'Hello, Marcus,' she said carefully, wondering how her voice sounded to him. Older and wiser? Or still full of youthful awe?

He moved into eyeshot—though heaven only knew

how long he'd been in earshot for. But he didn't look at Donna straight away. He was staring down at Tony Paxman, so that Donna was able to observe him without him noticing.

And, oh. Oh, oh, *oh*! Her heart thumped out of control before she could stop it.

She had known that she would see him again, and she had practised in her head for just this moment. Some devil deep in her heart had wondered if his hair might be thinning. If he had allowed his wealth and success to go to his stomach and piled on weight. Or if he might have developed some kind of stoop. Or started wearing hideous clothes which didn't suit him.

But he hadn't. Of course he hadn't.

Marcus Foreman was still the kind of man who most women would leave home for.

'Tony,' said Marcus easily.

The lawyer inclined his head. 'Marcus.'

'Do you two know each other?' Donna asked Tony in surprise.

'Oh, everybody knows Marcus,' he responded, with a shrug which didn't quite come off.

But Donna had detected a subtle change in her lunch companion. Suddenly Tony Paxman did not look or sound like the smooth, slick lawyer of earlier. He sounded like a very ordinary man. A man, moreover, who had just recognised the leader of the pack.

Marcus turned to her at last, and Donna realised that she now had the opportunity to react to him as she had always vowed she would react if she ever saw him again. Coolly and calmly and indifferently.

Her polite smile didn't slip, but she wondered if there was any way of telling from the outside that her heart-rate had just doubled. And that the palms of her hands were moist and sticky with sweat.

'So. Donna,' Marcus said slowly, and she met his dark-lashed eyes with reluctant fascination, their ice-blue light washing over her as pure and as clear as an early-morning swimming pool.

'So. Marcus,' she echoed faintly, eyes flickering over *him*. Okay, so he hadn't become bald or fat or ugly, but he'd certainly changed. Changed a lot. But hadn't they all?

'Do you want to say it, or shall I?' His voice was heavy with mockery, and something else. Something she couldn't quite put her finger on, but it told her to beware.

'Say what?'

'Long time no see,' he drawled lazily. 'Isn't that the kind of cliché that people usually come out with after this long?'

'I guess they do,' she said slowly, thinking that nine whole years had passed since she had seen him. How could that be? 'You could have said, "Hi, Donna—great to see you!" But that would have been a whacking great lie, wouldn't it, Marcus?'

'You said it.' He smiled. 'And you're the world's expert where lying is concerned, aren't you, Donna?'

Their gazes clashed and she found herself observing every tiny detail of his face; a face she'd once loved—but now she told herself that it was just a face.

She'd known him at the beginning of his rapid rise, before success had become as familiar to him as breathing. Before he'd had a chance to fashion himself in his own image, rather than one which had been passed down to him.

Gone was the buttoned down, clean-cut and preppie look which had been his heritage. The polished brogues and the perfectly knotted tie. The soft Italian leather shoes and the shirts made in Jermyn Street. The suit had gone, too. Now he wore pale trousers and a shirt. But a silk shirt, naturally. With—wonder of wonders—the two top buttons casually left undone. He looked sexy and sensational.

He had let his hair grow, too. A neatly clipped style had once defined the proud tilt of his head. Now strands of it licked at his eyebrows and kissed the high-boned structure of his cheeks. Stroked the back of his neck with loving, dark tendrils. He looked as rugged and as ruffled as if he'd just tumbled out of some beautiful girl's bed after an afternoon of wild sex.

Maybe he had.

Her smile froze as she found she could picture the scene all too clearly. Marcus with one of those long-legged thoroughbred type of girls wrapped around him. The kind who'd used to hang around waiting for him like groupies.

She searched in desperation for something cool and neutral to say, her gaze fixing with a pathetic kind of relief on his shoes. 'You're obviously not working.'

Only his eyes hadn't changed, and now they chased away faint surprise. As if her reaction had not been what he had expected. He glanced down at the navy deck shoes which covered his bare feet. 'What's wrong with them?' he demanded.

'Well, nothing really, I suppose. Just not the most conventional of footwear, is it?' she observed wryly. 'You look like you're about to go sailing, rather than running a business.'

'But I don't run a conventional business,' he growled impatiently. 'And I don't feel the need to hide behind a suit and tie any more.'

'My! What a little rebel you've become, Marcus!' commented Donna mildly, noticing the watchful spark which darkened his eyes from aquamarine to sapphire.

There was a small, apologetic cough from the table, and Donna and Marcus both started as Tony Paxman looked up at them. Donna bit her lip in vexation.

She'd forgotten all about her lunch partner! How rude of her! And how unimaginative, too. Just because Marcus Foreman had walked in, that didn't mean that the rest of the world had stopped turning.

It just seemed that way....

'Er, shall we order coffee, Tony?' she asked him quickly.

But Tony Paxman looked as if he'd taken about as much rejection as he could handle in one day. He shook his head as he rose to his feet—master of his own destiny once more as he made a big pantomime out of gazing at his watch.

'Heck! Is that the time? Time I wasn't here! Client meeting at three.' He held his hand out towards Donna and she took it guiltily. 'Thanks very much for lunch, Donna. I enjoyed it.'

Suddenly Donna felt bad. She hadn't meant for this to happen—for Marcus to disrupt her whole lunch, her whole *day*. Which left her wondering just what she *had* expected. She'd known that there was a strong possibility she would see him today. Had she naively supposed that he would pass by her table without a flicker of recognition? Or that they would exchange, at most, a hurried nod?

'Thanks for everything you've done, Tony! Maybe we'll do this another time.'

'Er, yes. Quite. Goodbye, Marcus.' Tony gave a grimace as Marcus clasped his fingers in what was obviously an enthusiastic handshake. 'Fantastic lunch! Wonderful food! As always.'

'Thanks very much,' murmured Marcus.

The two of them watched in silence while Tony Paxman threaded his way between the tables, and suddenly Donna felt almost light-headed as Marcus turned his head to study her. As though she'd just plunged into the swimming-pool-blue of his eyes without having a clue how to swim.

'Congratulations, Donna,' he offered drily. 'You've latched onto one of the town's wealthiest and brightest young lawyers.'

'His bank balance and his pretty face don't interest me—I chose him because he was the best.'

He raised his eyebrows. 'At what?'

'Not what you're obviously thinking! He was recommended to me,' she answered, with a sigh. But even as she said it she realised that she didn't have to justify herself to Marcus. Not any more. He wasn't her boss. He wasn't anything except the man who'd given her such a disastrous introduction into the world of lovemaking.

And then dumped her.

'And did the person who recommended him also tell you that he has just come through a mud-slinging divorce which was *very* nasty? That he's ready and available—but only if you don't mind half his salary going out on his ex-wife and two children? I know that financial embarrassment tends to put some women off.'

And then he gave a brief, unexpected smile which half blinded her. 'Heavens,' he murmured. 'I sounded almost *jealous* for a moment back there.'

'Yes, you did,' she agreed sweetly. 'But there's really

no need to be, Marcus—my relationship with Tony Paxman is strictly business.'

'I couldn't care less about your relationship with anyone!' He stared insolently at her fingers, which were bare of rings. 'But I presume that you *are* still in the marriage market?'

Donna stared at him. 'I'm still single, if that's what you mean by your charming question. How about you?'

'Yeah,' he said softly. 'Still single.' His eyes narrowed. 'So what are you doing back here, Donna? Are you planning on staying around?'

Was she willing to be interrogated by him? To lay herself open to his opinion and probably his criticism. 'I'd love to tell you about it, Marcus.' She smiled as she realised that there were a million and one things she could be legitimately occupying herself with. 'Pity I don't have the time right now.'

Something in her manner told him it wasn't true. But no surprises there. Hadn't she lied to him before? Only then he'd been too young and too blind with lust to see it. 'I bet it's nothing urgent,' he commented silkily. 'Nothing that can't wait.'

'But I might be rushing off to an urgent appointment,' she objected.

'Might be. But you're not,' he breathed, his voice thickening as he recalled the wasted opportunity of the one night he'd spent with her. 'You've got the pampered air of a woman who has taken the day off work.'

He pulled out the chair opposite her with a question in his eyes. 'So, why don't I join you for coffee now that your silver-tongued lawyer has flown?' he suggested softly. 'And then you can tell me exactly what you're doing here.'

CHAPTER TWO

DONNA was torn. Wanting to stay—because when Marcus was in a room it was as though someone had just switched on the lights. Even now. Yet also wanting to run out of the restaurant as fast as her feet would carry her.

And wouldn't that just convince him that she was still an emotional teenager where he was concerned?

Smoothing the cream silk dress down over her hips, she sat further back on her seat. 'Okay, then,' she answered coolly. 'I will.'

Marcus expelled a soft breath of triumph. He'd seen her hesitate before sliding that irresistible bottom back. So she had overridden her better judgement and decided to stay, had she? A pulse began to throb with slow excitement at his temple. The die had been cast. A smile curved the corners of his lips almost cruelly as he lowered his powerful frame into the chair facing her.

He gave a barely perceptible nod across the room at a watching waitress, and that was the coffee taken care of, then found himself in the firing line of a pair of eyes which were as green as newly mown grass. Eyes which these days were darkened with mascara which had teased the lashes into sooty spikes. Not the bare, pale lashes he'd always used to tease her about.

'You look completely different, Donna,' he observed slowly.

She gave him a disbelieving stare. 'Well, of course I do! I'm nine years older, for a start. People change.

Especially women.' And yet for a moment back there she had felt just like the unsophisticated teenager he obviously remembered. 'And I can't look *that* different,' she declared, in surprise. 'Seeing as you recognised me straight away.'

'Yeah.' Just from one, swift glance across a busy restaurant. He'd surprised himself. Maybe it had been the unforgettable fire of her hair. Or the curves of her body. Or that rope of amber beads at her throat—golden beads as big as pebbles. He swallowed as he remembered the only other time he had seen her wearing *those*. 'Maybe you're just printed indelibly on my mind,' he drawled.

'I *do* tend to have that effect on people,' she agreed, mock-seriously, and she could tell that her new-found sophistication surprised him.

Marcus might not know it, but he'd been largely responsible for her transformation from chambermaid to business woman. How many times had she planned to knock him dead if ever she saw him again? Well, now he was sitting just a few feet away from her. Was he *really* as indifferent to her as he appeared to be?

'So, how have I changed, Marcus?' she asked him sweetly.

He leaned back in the chair and took the opportunity to study her, which gave him far more pleasure than he felt comfortable with. Donna King had turned into a real little head-turner, he recognised wryly—despite her unconventional looks and her even more unconventional background.

He'd worked long enough in the high-octane world of upmarket restaurants to recognise that the deceptive simplicity of her cream silk dress would cost what most people earned in a month. As would those sexy high-heeled shoes he'd glimpsed as she'd slid her ankles beneath the table. Shoes like that cost money. He'd bet she had a handbag to match. He glanced at the floor to where, like most women, she had placed it, close to her feet. Yes, she did!

She was looking at him expectantly, and he remembered her question.

How had she changed?

'You used to look cheap,' he said honestly, not seeming to notice her frozen expression. 'Now you look expensive. A high-maintenance woman. With expensive tastes,' he added. 'So who pays for it, Donna? Who's the lucky man?'

Donna bristled. 'Heavens—but you're behind the times!' she scoffed. 'Women don't need to rely on men to pay for their finery, not these days. Everything I'm wearing I paid for myself!'

Marcus swallowed. Then it was money well spent.

Someone had threaded a cream satin ribbon though the fiery strands of her hair, sending out a seductive and confusing signal of schoolgirl sophistication. And her breasts were partially concealed behind a cleverly cut jacket. So that one moment he could see their erotic swell, only to have the jacket shield them when she moved her body slightly forward. It was maddening! He felt the intrusive jerk of desire, and willed it to go away.

'And you're wearing make-up,' he observed, almost accusingly. 'Yet you never used to wear a scrap!'

Donna laughed. 'Of course I didn't! When you get up at six in the morning to start stripping the beds, slapping on make-up is the very last thing on your mind. Believe me—a chambermaid's life doesn't lend itself very well to glamour.'

'Not unless you get lucky with the boss.'

She stared at him. 'But I didn't get lucky, did I,

Marcus? In fact the best bit of luck I had was having the courage to walk away from this place without a backward glance.'

'Yet you're here today?' he said bluntly. 'Why?'

'I'm celebrating.'

'How very intriguing,' he murmured. 'Shall I guess why, or are you going to tell me?'

Well, he would find out soon enough, whatever she said—and then he might sit up and wipe that smug smile off his face and take notice of something other than her body—which she noticed he hadn't stopped looking at.

Donna had opened her mouth to reply, when a very beautiful woman wearing a sleek black dress carried a tray of coffee over to their table.

Donna watched the woman's gleaming black head, with its perfectly symmetrical centre parting, as she set down the tiny cups and the cafetière in front of them, and the plate of thin almond biscuits. Then she heard her ask, 'Anything else for you, Marcus?' in a soft French accent, and noticed that she looked at him with politely concealed lust shining from her dark eyes.

'No, thanks!' He shook his head, his attention momentarily distracted as he watched the girl glide away.

'She seems very efficient,' observed Donna.

'Yes, she is.'

'And very good-looking.' Now why had she said *that*?

He raised his eyebrows. 'Very.'

'But not one of the waitresses—judging by her dress,' she probed.

He gave her a perplexed smile. 'Do you want to talk about my staff, Donna?'

'Of course not.'

He poured out the coffee, automatically offering Donna the sugar bowl, and she felt a little tug of nostalgia as she wondered whether he'd actually remembered her excessively sweet tooth.

'No, thanks. I've given up sugar in tea and coffee.'

'What, even when you're mysteriously celebrating?'

'It's no mystery.' She sipped her coffee and smiled. 'That's the reason I was having lunch with Tony Paxman, if you really want to know. I've just tied up a deal.'

'What kind of deal is that?'

She heard the condescension in his voice and her determination not to be smug or triumphant threatened to fly out of the window. But she hauled it back. 'A business deal,' she told him coolly. 'Which I happen to have set up.' She sat back in her chair and waited to hear what he would say.

He frowned at her, looking as puzzled as if she'd just announced she was running for mayor. 'You mean you're going to be working for someone else?'

'What a predictable and irritating conclusion to jump to! Actually, I'm going to be working for myself.' Donna even allowed herself a smile. 'I'm the boss.'

His hand stilled only briefly on its path to the sugar bowl, and he picked a cube up between his fingers, dipped it into his coffee and bit into it. 'Doing what?'

She savoured the moment like a hot bath at the end of a long, hard day. 'Running a restaurant, actually,' she answered serenely.

'Where?'

'Right here in Winchester.'

His interest was stirred, along with his imagination. It was far too close to home to be mere coincidence, surely? The same business, in the same *town*.

So why?

Was she seeking revenge for what had happened all

those years ago? Or was her extraordinary decision to come back based on a far more basic urge? Had that last night left a dark, demon blot on her memory, as it had on his?

Did she want...? Marcus felt the sweet, slow throbbing of sexual excitement begin... Did she want to play out that scene once more—only this time with a far more mutually satisfactory ending?

'Well, you really must have come along by leaps and bounds, Donna,' he mused, 'if you're planning a capital venture on a chambermaid's salary.'

If the remark had been made in order to inflame, then it served its purpose. 'Do I *look* like a chambermaid?' she demanded.

His groin ached. No. Right now she looked as he had never imagined she could look. Beautiful and proud and refined and, well...classy.

'Do I?' she persisted.

'No,' he growled. 'But that's what you were the last time I saw you.' His eyes narrowed. 'It makes me wonder what you've been doing in the intervening years to put you in the position of being able to buy a restaurant.'

'What do you *think* I've been doing? No—don't bother answering that! I'll tell you! I happen to have worked extremely hard since you kicked me out on the street!'

'Spare me the Victorian imagery,' he sighed. 'I gave you a generous pay-off *and* a job in London to go to. You were the one who decided not to accept.'

'I didn't want anything more to do with you!' she said bitterly.

He shrugged. 'That was your prerogative—but I refuse to be cast in the role of unfeeling bastard just because it suits your story!'

Donna glared. 'I managed very well on my own, thank you. I travelled to New Zealand and cooked on a sheep station. I worked in a bar in Manhattan—*and* on a cruise-liner! I know the hotel and restaurant industry inside out. I worked hard and saved hard—'

'And played hard, too, I imagine?' he cut in.

'That's something you'll never know!' She stared at him curiously across the table—expecting him to show *some* kind of reaction. But there was none. Just that barely interested, faintly bored expression.

'Well, I shan't be losing any sleep over it,' he offered drily, as he stirred his coffee. 'It's a precarious profession. I see new restaurants going under all the time.'

'Thanks for the few words of encouragement!'

'That's a fact, not a scare story. You know what they say—if you can't stand the heat then get out of the kitchen!' He gave a slow smile. 'Want to tell me all about it, Donna—or are you worried about industrial espionage?'

'No, my only worry is that I might lose my temper!'

He laughed, enjoying the hidden fires of conflict, and his smile sent her blood pressure soaring. 'Feel free,' he murmured.

Ignoring the sultry innuendo, Donna paused for effect. 'I've bought The Buttress Guest House!' she announced.

Marcus narrowed his eyes. So. Not just in the same town, but on the same street. Neighbours as well as rivals? He hid a smile. Not really. No one in their right mind would dream of comparing a run-down boarding house to a five-star hotel! 'You're opening up a *guest* house?'

'That's not what I said,' she contradicted. 'I've bought it and converted it.'

Of course she had, thought Marcus, as all the facts began to slot into place.

The Buttress Guest House had gone bankrupt a couple of years ago and no one had wanted to touch it. It was small and it was tired—with tiny, impractical rooms and, more importantly, no parking facilities.

But recently the house had seen a plumber's van parked outside it for the best part of a month. Painters and decorators and French-polishers had been employed to work there. Hammers and drills had been heard as you walked past. Interesting pieces of furniture had been seen disappearing into the beautiful old house.

Marcus, along with most other people in the town, had assumed that the house was being converted back to a private residence before being put on the property market again. Now it seemed he'd been wrong.

'You've *converted* it,' he breathed, and stared at her assessingly. 'Into what?'

'A tea-room, actually.'

'A tea-room?'

'That's what I said!'

He very nearly laughed, but something in the proud way she'd said it stopped him. 'How quaint,' he murmured.

'I'll take that as a compliment.'

'It wasn't supposed to be a compliment.' He frowned, and instead of feeling angry he felt a maddening rush of the protectiveness she'd always used to bring out in him. 'Have you taken any business advice, Donna? Seriously?'

'If only you knew just how insulting that question sounded! Or maybe you do! Of course I took advice! *And* I did accounting at night school!' Her eyes narrowed suspiciously. 'Why?'

'Because there's no parking for any cars, that's why!' he exploded. 'Didn't it occur to you to ask why the place had been on the market for so long? Or did you think it was a bargain, just waiting for you to breeze along and buy it?'

'For your information, I don't need any parking!'

'Oh, really?'

'Yes, really! The property happens to be on the route of at least two official Winchester Walks. The tourist office know all about me. They're going to help get me started and I'm hoping that word of mouth will do the rest. People won't need cars—and that's the kind of customer I want! People who are interested in history and sightseeing, and can be bothered to walk down the road for a cup of tea and a piece of cake instead of polluting the atmosphere in some horrible gas-guzzling machine!'

There was silence.

'You're crazy!' he said at last. 'Crazy and impetuous!'

'What's the matter?' She gave him a steady, cool look. 'Do you think that being my own boss is too good for someone of *my* pedigree?'

'What your mother did for a living didn't concern me,' he said coldly. 'But the fact that you deceived me did. But then our whole relationship was built on a tissue of lies, wasn't it?'

'Relationship?' she scorned. 'Oh, come *on*, Marcus! To describe what we shared as a "relationship" is not only inaccurate—it's insulting to relationships!'

He sat back in his chair and studied her, the ice-blue eyes as cool as she had ever seen them. 'So tell me—is this whole enterprise of yours some naive plan for revenge?'

Donna blinked at him in genuine astonishment. 'Revenge?'

'It's a natural progression, if you stop to think about it,' he mused. 'You striking out, in a primitive kind of way, to make me pay for what happened between us.'

For a moment she was dumbfounded, and it took a few incredulous seconds before she could speak. 'Marcus—please credit me with a little more intelligence than that. I'm not stupid enough to set myself up to be miserable—and pursuing some sort of vendetta against you would make anyone miserable.'

'Maybe being miserable is a price worth paying.' He shrugged. 'Depends how badly you want to pay me back!'

She gave him a look of undiluted amazement, realising that maybe he didn't know her at all. 'What a disgustingly over-inflated ego you have, Marcus! Do you really think that I would stake everything I own on a venture like this unless I thought I could make some kind of success of it?'

'I have no idea. Maybe I've misjudged you,' he said, sounding as though he didn't think he had at all. 'But in that case—how did you manage to keep it so quiet for so long?' he mused. 'And why?'

'How?' She smiled. 'I hired a good lawyer. You said yourself that Tony Paxman was expensive. Well, he's good—and you always get what you pay for—that's something else I've learnt. As for why...' She met his gaze steadily. 'I suspected that you might try and block the sale if you knew who was behind it.'

And she was right—damn her! Not because he feared competition—he'd always been able to deal with *that*. No, it was more to do with the effect she had on him... Marcus was silent as he dragged oxygen into his body and fought to swamp his instincts. He felt unwelcome

heat invade him. She always made him want what he
didn't need...

Seconds ticked by as his heart thundered and the tiny
hairs on the back of his neck stung like pin-pricks. He
didn't speak. Didn't dare to. Not until he was sure that
his feelings were under control once more. Only then
did he speak, lacing his words with sarcasm. 'So, it's
open warfare, is it, Donna?' he drawled.

'Of course not! I'm sure there's room for both of us,'
she said mock-generously. 'People will choose where
they want to eat.'

'As you did today,' he remarked obscurely. 'But
maybe you had your own special reasons for wanting to
eat here.'

Donna held her breath. 'Like what?'

'Like me.'

'*You?*'

'Mmm. Me. There are plenty of other places you
could have taken your lawyer to. Maybe you just
couldn't wait to see me again.'

It was partly true—but not for the reasons he was
implying, that she was still vulnerable where he was concerned. Seeing Marcus again had been intended to be
the final proof that not only had she turned her life
around, but she had succeeded in forgetting the man who
had brought her nothing but heartache.

Donna opened her mouth without thinking, and the
words came fizzing out before she could take them back.
'And why would I want to see you again, Marcus? Why
would I want to re-acquaint myself with a man who gave
me nothing but grief? The man who strode in and took
exactly what he wanted and found he couldn't handle it
afterwards! Was that the real reason you sacked me,
Marcus—not because I'd lied to you, but because I re-

minded you of what you'd done? Were you feeling guilty that you'd seduced a poor little virgin?'

'You're talking like a victim, Donna—and I can assure you that you were nothing of the kind. For an innocent you certainly knew how to be provocative.' His mouth tightened as he lowered his voice. 'As for seduction—that's too fine a word to describe what was a very regrettable incident all round.'

'A "very regrettable incident"?' she repeated in disbelief. 'My God—I'm going to enjoy becoming the most popular eaterie in town! I hope all your clients come flocking to *me*!'

He gave a sad shake of his head as he rose to his feet. 'Oh, Donna,' he sighed. 'You may be older—but you don't seem to have acquired a lot of wisdom along the way. Your hare-brained scheme won't work. Believe me.'

'Only time will tell!'

His smile was wry. 'I'll try very hard not to gloat when my prediction comes true.'

'And I'll be laughing all the way to the bank when it doesn't!'

'We'll see.' He tore his eyes away from that riveting glimpse of her breasts and walked out of the restaurant, leaving Donna and just about every other female in the room staring wide-eyed after him.

CHAPTER THREE

DONNA paid her bill and then made her way out of the restaurant, trying not to notice that people were staring and wondering if it was because she'd been sitting with Marcus.

It had not been the meeting she'd fantasised about. She *had* been naive. *And* stupid. Imagining that all those sparks of sexual attraction would have been extinguished over the years.

Outside, the afternoon sunshine was beginning to fade, and a tiny breeze had blown up which made her shiver, turning her flesh to goosebumps beneath the cream silk jacket.

She turned and walked up the street towards her newly purchased future, her high-heeled shoes clipping over the familiar pavements until she stopped outside The Buttress and looked up at it. At the worn, wooden door and the ancient brick—all warm and terracotta-coloured in the dying light of the sun. Hers.

The new sign would be erected tomorrow, and the notices would go out in all the trade press. The tea-room had been dominating her thoughts for so long now. She'd been bubbling over with excitement about all her plans and hopes for it—but seeing Marcus today had made her confront the fact that he still had the power to affect her in a way that no other man had ever come close to.

She felt the beat of her heart, heavy and strong, as she remembered the way he looked. Different. Older and rougher round the edges. All tousled and tough—and radiating an earthy sexuality she knew she was incompatible with.

The first time she had met him he'd been kind to her. Kind and caring, yes—but in the way that a Victorian benefactor might throw a bone to a starving dog...

As a teenager, Donna had arrived in Winchester on a rainy December day, dressed in jeans and a jumper and a worn tweed jacket she'd picked up at a car-boot sale and which had been too thin to withstand the constant drizzle. She'd been soaked. Her face had been bare of make-up, her lashes matted with raindrops and her hair a wild ginger mess frizzing all the way down down her back.

There had only been one week to go until Christmas, and there'd been fairy-lights threaded everywhere: outside all the shops and pubs, woven into the bare branches of the trees—their colours blurred like jewels through the grey of the relentless rain.

As she'd turned the corner into Westgate street Donna had seen the welcoming blaze of The New Hampshire hotel and had shivered. It was the sort of place you usually only saw in story books—a beautiful, elegant old building, with two bay trees standing in dark, shiny boxes outside. The windows were sparkly-clean and the paintwork gleamed. It was the kind of place which reeked of money. You could tell just by looking. And places like this were always looking for seasonal workers.

Clutching onto her holdall with frozen fingers, she'd pushed the glass doors open and walked into the foyer, where a man had been standing at the top of a ladder, positioning a huge silver star on top of a Christmas tree whose tip was brushing against the high ceiling.

Donna had quietly slid her holdall onto the thick carpet and watched him. He'd been wearing dark trousers, which had looked new and neatly pressed, and his shirt had been exquisitely made. Quality clothes on a quality body.

She had waited until the star was firmly in place. 'Bravo!' she cheered, and he looked over his shoulder, frowned, then came slowly down the ladder to face her.

His hair was thick and dark and tapered neatly into his neck, and his eyes were the most extraordinary colour she had ever seen. Icy and pale. Clear and blue. As if they had been washed clean. And Donna felt the first tiptoeing of an emotion she simply didn't recognise.

He frowned again as he looked her up and down, and his voice matched his clothes. Rich. 'Can I help you?'

The implication being that he couldn't. That she was in the wrong place. The story of her life, really. She decided to brazen it out.

'Do you have a room?'

The surprise in his eyes was gone almost as quickly as it had appeared, and he shrugged his shoulders apologetically. 'I'm sorry. I'm afraid we're fully booked. It's our busiest time of year and—'

'Actually, I don't want a room,' she interrupted quickly, thinking that it was nice of him to pretend that she could afford a room in a hotel when it was pretty obvious she couldn't. 'I'm looking for work.'

His eyes narrowed. 'What kind of work?'

'Anything. You name it—I can do it! I can wait tables—'

He shook his head. 'I'm sorry. We're a silver-service restaurant,' he said politely.

'Or peel potatoes?'

He smiled. 'We have our full complement of kitchen staff.'

'Oh.' She pursed her lips together to stop them wobbling and went to pick up her holdall. 'Okay. Fair enough. Merry Christmas!'

The man sighed. 'Now you're making me feel like Scrooge.'

'You don't look like Scrooge.' She grinned. Too cute by far.

He thought how thin her cheeks looked. And how pale. 'Ever done any work as a chambermaid?'

'No. But I learn fast.'

'How old are you?'

'Nearly twenty.' The words were out before she could stop them, and she told herself that it wasn't a lie, merely an exaggeration. Because she also told herself that this man was the kind of man who would try to send her home if he knew she was barely eighteen.

And then where would she go?

'Been travelling?' he asked, flicking a pale blue glance over at the holdall, then at the worn elbows of her jacket.

'Kind of.'

She had been moving around for most of her young life. She liked it that way. It meant that she didn't have to give away too much about herself. But she could see him looking at her curiously and knew she ought to say *something*.

'Bit of a nomad, that's me,' she explained with a smile—wondering what had possessed her to add, 'My mother was an actress. We moved around a lot when I was a child.'

'Oh, I see.' He nodded, wondering what he was letting himself in for. But through the glass doors he could see that the rain was now lashing down, to form lake-sized puddles on the pavement outside. It was the kind of night you wouldn't throw a dog out into. 'I'll take you on until the New Year. But no longer—do you understand?'

'Oh, thanks!' Donna breathed, looking for a moment as though she was about to fling her arms around him.

Marcus took a hasty step back.

She wasn't the kind of woman he would normally find attractive in a million years—with her curly ginger hair and pale eyelashes and freckles.

But there was something indomitable about her. Something that made her look small and tough and brave. Something feisty, which was oddly attractive and made him feel strange and warm and prickly inside.

'Don't mention it,' he growled. 'What's your name?'

'It's Donna. Donna King. What's yours?'

'Marcus Foreman.'

She lifted her shoulders in a tiny questioning movement. 'Should I call you Mr Foreman?'

It was such a sweetly old-fashioned proposition that he almost laughed, then checked himself in time. He didn't want her thinking he was making fun of her. 'You're only a year younger than me.' He smiled gently, not noticing her wince. 'Marcus will do just fine.'

'Marcus,' she said shyly. 'Are you the boss?'

It took a moment for him to answer. 'Yes,' he said abruptly. He still couldn't quite get used to the fact that this place was now his. But then his father had only been dead a year. He looked down at her and his features softened.

Her face was so pale that her freckles stood out like tiny brown stars, and her cheekbones looked much too sharp. She could do with a little fleshing out. 'Have you eaten?'

Donna's eyes grew wary. Could he tell? That she hadn't seen a square meal in getting on for a week? And what kind of conclusions would he draw from that?

He watched her reaction and was reminded of a stray cat his mother had once let him keep. The creature had been starving, yet stubborn—mistrusting any attempts at kindness—and Marcus had learnt that the only way to handle that cat was to seem not to care. He shrugged, sounding as if she could take it or leave it. 'There's plenty of food here if you want some.'

'Okay.' She shrugged too. 'Might as well.'

He took her down to the kitchen and introduced her to the staff, and then found things to keep him occupied while she ate and he watched her out of the corner of his eye.

He had never seen anyone eat with so much greed, or so much hunger. Especially a woman. Yet she didn't tear at the food like an animal. Hers was a graceful greed. She savoured every single mouthful with pleasure—and when she'd finally finished she wiped her mouth delicately with a napkin, like some sort of princess, and beamed him a smile.

And that smile pierced Marcus's armour like a ray of sunshine hitting a sheet of ice.

As spring slid into early summer, Marcus showed no sign of asking her to leave. And Donna heaved a huge sigh of relief, because she loved the town and she loved the hotel and she wanted to stay.

She loved the grey flint walls of the ancient buildings and the sound of the choristers' voices spilling their pure, sweet notes into the scented air around the cathedral square. She loved the lush green and crystal streams of the water meadows, where you could walk for miles and feel that you'd stepped back a century. And maybe more than a bit of her loved Marcus, too. Who wouldn't?

It was the first place that had felt like home for a long time. Maybe ever.

She made herself indispensable by working as hard as possible. And Donna could work. If there was one thing her childhood had taught her it was that you didn't get anything for nothing.

Her mother had been a stripper—spending her nights performing in run-down theatres along the coast and her days mostly sleeping. In a way, Donna had brought herself up—making herself as invisible as she knew how. Because a little girl had fitted uneasily into the kind of life her mother had chosen.

She knew that Marcus's father had died the year before, and one day she plucked up enough courage to ask him what had happened to his mother.

Mistake!

The icy-blue eyes narrowed suspiciously. 'Why?'

'I j-just wondered.'

'She's been dead for a long time,' he snapped.

She thought that it was an odd way to put it. As though a chapter of his own life had come to an end with his mother's death. Maybe it had.

'And how old were you?' she asked.

He scowled at the intrusion. 'I was nine, and, yes— before you make the obvious response—it *was* awful. Okay? And I don't want to talk about it. Okay?'

End of subject. But Donna was relieved, in a funny kind of way. The kind of person who didn't like to explain was also the kind of person who didn't ask too many questions. Although it wasn't as if a man like Marcus would be interested in one of his chambermaids, was it?

But sometimes she caught him watching her, when he thought she wasn't looking. And sometimes he even let his guard down enough to laugh at something she said. And sometimes he would tease her about her pale eyelashes, and the way she used to nibble the tip of her thumb when she was nervous.

One day he found her in the staffroom, playing cards with one of the waiters, and he challenged her to play. Only to discover that she could beat him at every card game he'd ever learnt.

Marcus was a man who admired expertise in whatever field it was demonstrated, and he seemed to look at her in a completely different light after that. He told her that watching her shuffle the cards was like poetry in motion, and Donna beamed with pleasure at the praise.

'Where ever did you learn to play like that?' he questioned.

'Oh, here and there,' she told him airily. 'You don't want to know.'

'No, you're right. I don't!' he laughed.

And it was at times like these that Donna had to remind herself that there were some men you should never start getting attracted to, on account of who they were.

And Marcus Foreman was one of them.

He had a younger brother called Lucas, who was nearly as good-looking as his brother, but foxy in a way that Marcus wasn't foxy. And blond, not dark. He was a photographer, of sorts, and he was away travelling, somewhere in Thailand, He hadn't even bothered coming back for Christmas. But Marcus didn't seem to mind.

The first time Donna met Lucas she was on her hands and knees brushing up some crumbs from behind a large pot plant on the first-floor landing, when she heard a low wolf whistle from behind her.

She whirled round, bashing her elbow in the process, and saw a man with blue eyes who looked like a fallen angel. She recognised the likeness immediately. 'You must be Lucas!' she cried.

'And you must be a hallucination,' he murmured, licking his bottom lip like an old-fashioned villian. 'Wow! Stand up. Go on!'

He was the boss's brother. So Donna did as he asked and rose to her feet, not much liking the smile on his face as he looked her up and down as if he'd never seen a woman before.

'Oh, my word!' he breathed softly. 'No wonder big brother wasn't crazy about me coming home—he obviously wanted to keep a living, breathing Barbie doll all to himself!'

'Stay away from her, Lucas—do you hear that?' came a soft command, and Marcus walked up behind his brother as soundlessly as a wraith, silently cursing himself for the attractive enticement having Donna King around the place was proving to be. Those scruffy clothes she'd arrived in had done a remarkable job of concealing a body which regular meals and regular sleep had transformed into something resembling a centrefold.

She was as bright as a button, too. Hard-working. Friendly. And considerate—from what little he knew of her. And he deliberately kept it as little as he could. Knowledge equalled understanding, and understanding could lead on to all kinds of unwanted things.

And whilst Marcus was honest enough to admit that he fancied the pants off Donna King—he was also honest enough to realise that they were worlds apart. Worlds.

Lucas shot Donna a search-*me* kind of look. 'Marcus likes playing the big macho bit!' he grinned.

'Leave that now, will you please, Donna?' snapped Marcus, because she had bent over to flick up the last few crumbs of dust.

'But—'

'Just *leave* it!'

Donna straightened up and smoothed down the pale green uniform which strained so horribly over her bust, slotting the brush onto the dustpan before looking up at Marcus and smiling. 'Are we still on for a game later?'

Lucas's pupils dilated. 'A game of *what*?'

'Not tonight,' said Marcus tightly. 'Just go *away*, Donna, will you? I want to talk to Lucas in private!'

Afterwards, Marcus realised that the worst thing he could possibly have done was to warn Lucas off the luscious chambermaid. His wayward brother loved nothing more than a slice of forbidden fruit.

But what alternative did he have? He didn't think for a moment that she was an unsullied young virgin—but for all Donna's worldliness she had a curious and refreshing innocence about her.

It was a potent combination—and one which caused him to lie awake at night, aching and sweating and pressing his groin hard against the mattress, as if he was trying to punish himself.

Donna saw how different the two brothers were. Marcus was the serious one, with all the responsibilities of the hotel weighing heavily on his shoulders. Lucas was simply devil-may-care. While Marcus seemed reluctant to find out anything about her Lucas wanted to know everything. And a little bit more besides.

But his openness made up for his inquisitiveness. He was so forthcoming—not like his brother at all. Through Lucas she heard about their childhood. About their wild

and beautiful mother—so different from their steady, unimaginative father.

Lucas was candid to the point of indiscretion, Donna
realised. He seemed unfazed by telling her of his
mother's infidelities and the ensuing rows. He explained
that his father had been too much in thrall to his spectacular wife to ever leave her.

He told her things which in her heart she knew should
have remained secret—and maybe that was why she told
Lucas the truth about *her* mother.

He didn't look at all shocked, merely looked her up
and down and said, 'Yes. I can see exactly why she was
a stripper, if her body was anything like yours.'

She could have bitten her tongue out and tossed it
away. 'But you won't tell Marcus?' she begged him.

His eyes were sly. 'Why not?'

'Please!'

'Okay,' he replied easily. 'Don't want to shock my
uptight big brother, do we?' The sly look returned. 'He
likes you, doesn't he?'

Donna shook her head. 'Only as a card partner,' she
said, fervently trying to convince herself.

'I don't think so,' said Lucas. 'He used to play bridge
with the local vicar, and he never used to look at *him*
like that!'

Lucas was pointing out nothing that Donna hadn't noticed for herself. Marcus really *did* seem to like her. That
look in his eyes sometimes…an intense kind of longing
that made her wonder why on earth he didn't just throw
caution to the wind, take her in his arms and…

She knew exactly why. They weren't equals. He was
the boss and she was the chambermaid and she should
never forget that. Because Marcus never did.

Donna saw the hotel grow more and more popular.

Everyone wanted to eat there, and it became the place to see and be seen in. Actors and media-types often drove down from London for dinner and a luxurious bed for the night.

One night a famous restaurant critic from a national newspaper came to review the restaurant. Every member of staff worked their socks off, and they all held their breath until the first edition claimed that it was the 'best-kept secret in the South of England'!

Not for long!

The reservations phone didn't stop ringing, and Marcus announced that he would be providing a meal in the private function room upstairs—to thank all the staff for their hard work.

Donna wore the only thing she had which was suitable—a black velvet dress she'd bought at a thrift shop. It was much too old and too severe for her, but it made her figure look absolutely show-stopping. She wore it with a necklace of huge amber beads which matched the colour of her hair exactly.

She drank champagne and let her hair down—literally and figuratively. In between courses she joined the chefs and waiters and shimmied around the room to the music which played in the background, knowing that Marcus was watching her.

And Donna was her mother's daughter. Whether or not the dancing was learned or inherited—she could dance like a dream.

Marcus couldn't take his eyes off her. He'd never wanted anyone or anything so badly, and once the coffee had been served he gave up trying to resist and slid into the seat next to her.

'Hello, Donna.' He smiled.

'Hello.'

They stared at one another.

'Enjoying yourself?'

'Mmm!' She was now!

He touched one of the pebble-sized amber beads she wore around her neck with the tip of his finger. 'These are beautiful,' he said softly. 'Who gave them to you?'

'My mother.'

'She has excellent taste.'

Donna smiled. 'Actually, she thought they were plastic—that's why she gave them to me. Funny, really—they were the only valuable piece of jewellery she owned, if only she'd known it. She used to walk around quite happily wearing paste.'

'And where's your mother now?' he amazed himself by asking. 'Playing Shakespeare somewhere?'

She wrinkled her nose, not wanting to talk about anything—especially not the stories she'd invented. She just wanted him to kiss her. 'Oh, she's given up acting now! She's running a bed and breakfast on the coast.'

'Whereabouts?'

Donna narrowed her eyes and gave a cynical laugh. 'Oh, nowhere you'll ever go, Marcus.'

The laugh made a hollow sort of sound, and Marcus suddenly caught a glimpse of another world. He saw it all. Seaside rock and greasy eggs on a plate. Ferris wheels and screams and the overpowering smell of chips. And he wanted no part of that world.

If only he didn't want Donna quite so much...

'You look...' His eyes roved over the clinging black velvet and he became temporarily lost for words.

The smile and the way he was watching her made her throw every bit of caution to the wind. She gazed at him provocatively over the top of her champagne glass. 'How do I look, Marcus?' she purred.

'Absolutely bloody gorgeous,' he said honestly.

'Gosh! That good?' Donna wanted him, ached for him, loved him. She knew she would never get another opportunity like this. She leaned forward to softly plant a kiss on his mouth.

He very nearly pulled her into his arms right there and then, until he remembered just in time that almost every member of his staff was watching.

'Let's save that for later,' he whispered.

'Save what?' she teased, automatically slipping into the flirtatious banter she had grown up listening to.

Pulse-points began to throb in places he hadn't even known had a pulse. 'That depends. What say we start with a kiss and see how we get on?'

'Mmm!' She giggled. 'Tell me when you're ready!'

But he noticed that she didn't bite the tip of her thumb the way she normally did when she was nervous. She was twenty years old, for heaven's sake! He wasn't planning on breaking any laws. She liked him and he liked her. He had grown to trust her. Life was too damned short. And you only got one bite of the cherry...

'Oh, I will,' he murmured, and their eyes locked in an unspoken promise. 'You can bet your life on it, sugar!'

When Donna escaped to the loo, she noticed that her face was flushed and that her eyes glittered like a rich woman's diamonds. She patted her wrists with cold water, and smoothed down the wild red tumble of her curls, and was just making her way back along the corridor towards the dining room when a figure slipped out from the shadows.

'Donna!'

Donna started, thinking at first that it was Marcus— until she noticed that the figure was slighter, the shoulders less broad. His voice wasn't so deep, either. 'Lucas!' she breathed, and slapped her palm over her thundering heart. 'You made me jump!'

He looked foxier than ever in the half-light. 'Pretty edgy, aren't you?' he observed. 'My brother has been sniffing round you like a dog all night.'

Donna frowned. 'Lucas, are you drunk?'

'A little. Not drunk enough.' He looked up at the ornate ceiling and scowled. 'Save me from claustrophobia—I need to get out of this place. Lend me some money, Donna.'

'No way! You haven't paid me back the last lot yet!' She made to walk on, but he stopped her.

'Don't you think it might blow things for you if he were to ever find out the truth about you?' he asked her casually.

She stilled. 'Wh-what are you talking about?'

He shrugged. 'The fact that you never knew your father. That your mother stripped for a living. That you spent your life moving around and dodging debts.' He paused for effect. 'Marcus is a very conventional man, Donna. He wouldn't just be shocked, he would be appalled. Do you want me to go on?'

'Are you trying to *blackmail* me, Lucas?'

He laughed. 'Oh, don't be so melodramatic! I'm just asking you a favour, that's all—just as you're expecting me to be discreet!'

She stared at him, her heart sinking as she realised that he could ruin everything. 'How much do you want?'

'Not much. Twenty will do.'

'Wait here.' She sighed, knowing that she probably wouldn't see the money again, but right now it didn't seem important. Nothing did except Marcus. 'I'll go and get my purse.'

When she walked back into the dining room she saw Marcus sitting alone at a table, watching her intently as she crossed the room towards him. And she never gave Lucas another thought.

Marcus was fighting a losing battle with his conscience, and in the end he gave up trying. He went back to her room and the sight of the cramped quarters only intensified his guilt. But the sight of Donna stretched out naked on the beaten gold of the bedspread almost made him lose his mind with desire.

But the act of making love was a disaster—painful and uncomfortable for her, and over far too quickly for him.

He lay awake, staring up through the dark at the ceiling, suspecting that Donna was feigning sleep beside him, but he found he couldn't face talking to her. It was the first time in his life that he had ever failed at anything, but he found that he had no desire to give her the pleasure he knew her beautiful body deserved.

It was supposed to have been a casual fling, nothing more. So why the hell had she kept her virginity a secret? He would have run a mile had he known.

Sliding out of bed, he pulled on his jeans and T-shirt and went down to the kitchen for a glass of milk. And Lucas was there, looking slightly the worse for wear as he flipped the top off a bottle of beer.

Lucas smiled. 'So, did you get your leg over with her?'

Marcus played dumb. 'Who?'

'Donna. Careful there, Marcus—she nearly qualifies as jail-bait!'

Marcus froze. 'She's twenty.'

'She's only eighteen.' Lucas swigged some beer and

his eyes narrowed with mischief. 'Did you know her mother was a stripper?'

It was the final straw, and the excuse that Marcus had been looking for.

Next day, he sacked her.

Donna put the key in the lock and looked down the road. From here she could see the lights of The New Hampshire quite clearly, looking as warm and as welcoming as on that first day, when she had glimpsed it shining like a beacon through the rain.

If Marcus had been standing at the window of *his* office, they could almost have waved at one another.

Not that there was much chance of that happening.

It had made perfect sense to come back here. The ideal spot and the ideal business opportunity—yet now she was wondering how she could have left such a huge factor as Marcus Foreman out of the equation.

She'd somehow thought that his attraction would have dimmed over the years. Well, she'd been wrong. Badly wrong.

The question was what she did about it. Could she ignore him? Act as if he didn't exist?

A cloud crossed over the sun and Donna shivered as she unlocked the front door with a very real sense of something unfinished hanging over her.

CHAPTER FOUR

DURING the next week, Donna was so busy with preparations for the opening of her tea-room that she was able to put Marcus on the back burner of her mind. There were so many different things to organise—flowers to order and staff to settle in and publicity to sort out—and through it all the telephone didn't seem to stop ringing.

She was sitting in her broom cupboard of an office, drawing tiny little teapots on the menus, when there was a rap at the door and a girl with dark curly hair stuck her head round.

'Donna?'

'Yes, Sarah—come in.' Donna smiled at her newest member of staff. 'I can't believe we open tomorrow. Tell me I'm not dreaming!'

'You're not dreaming,' answered Sarah obediently. 'Oh, and Mrs Armstrong—'

Donna blinked. 'Who?'

'The Mayor's wife. She's just phoned to say that they'd both be delighted to come tomorrow. So I've added them to the list.'

'Good. Let's hope we can fit them all in!'

Sarah moved forward and leaned over the desk to lower her voice, like someone about to break bad news. 'Oh, and by the way—there's a man in reception who says he wants to see you!'

'That'll be the photographer from the *Hampshire Times*,' answered Donna absently, thinking how chic the young waitress looked in her pale shell-coloured uniform.

Sarah Flowers had been broke and hungry and eager to learn—just as Donna herself had been all those years ago. In fact she'd deliberately advertised for staff in one of the city's free newspapers, as well as in local shop windows. It meant that she'd ended up with staff who really needed the work—and people who needed to work worked hardest. No one knew that better than Donna.

She glanced down at her watch, and frowned. 'He's a bit early, isn't he? I thought he wasn't supposed to be coming until after lunch.'

'It isn't the photographer,' said Sarah, in an odd, strangled sort of voice.

'Well, who is it, then?'

'Marcus something-or-other.' Sarah screwed up her face with concentration, then dimpled her cheeks as she remembered. 'Marcus Foreman!'

Donna felt her complacency slip. 'Tell him I'm busy. We open tomorrow.'

'I know. I already told him that—but he says he's not leaving until you see him.'

'Oh, does he?' Donna rose to her feet, see-sawing between exasperation and a definite sense of excitement. Because she had been expecting this. Half-dreading it and half-wanting it more than she could remember wanting anything for a long time. Though she hadn't stopped to ask herself why.

She quickly checked her appearance in the mirror which hung on the back of the door, and walked through to the foyer, where Marcus was sprawled on one of the leather sofas. He'd been reading the pink financial pages of one of the broadsheets, but he lowered it onto his chest as she walked in and stood in front of him, her arms crossed protectively over her breasts.

He didn't move an inch, just sat there looking at her with the sort of slow deliberation you might expect from a bloodstock expert seeing a racehorse for the first time.

Marcus had been wondering why he'd been unable to resist the compulsion to come across the road to see this place for himself. Now he knew that the reason was standing directly in front of him. Sweet Lord, but she looked sexy! But schoolmistressy sexy. All buttoned up and covered up in a plain chocolate-brown dress, with just the simple string of amber beads around her neck.

Had her legs always been that long? he wondered distractedly. Or did it have something to do with the three-inch heels which made them seem to reach all the way up to her armpits? And who else could have scraped their hair back as tightly as that and still manage to look good?

But then, Donna King had always managed to break a few rules where looks were concerned, he thought. Hell—he had found her desirable when she had breezed around the place with frizzy hair and no make-up.

'Hello, Marcus,' said Donna calmly, though calm was hardly the way she felt inside. She felt as if there was a nest of vipers wriggling around in the pit of her stomach. She felt squirmy and distracted and odd. 'This is an unexpected pleasure.'

'Say that once more with feeling,' he mocked.

She gave him a prim, I'm-going-to-humour-you smile. 'I'm afraid I haven't got time to see you at the moment. Really.'

He rose silently to his feet and she noticed that even with her highest heels on he still towered over her like a giant. 'Then make time,' he said softly.

She met the challenge in his eyes. 'Or what?'

'Or I'll sit here and distract you all day.'

'I would ignore you.'

'No, you wouldn't. But you could try.'

And she would probably fail. Because a man who looked like Marcus looked would be pretty impossible to ignore.

Today he was wearing some kind of charcoal-coloured silk shirt with a pair of black denims. And while some men never looked good in jeans once they had passed the age of twenty-one Marcus was not among them. She guessed that most twenty-one-year-olds would die to own a body like his!

'Come on, Donna,' he cajoled softly. 'Call it simple professional interest. I only want to see what you've got on offer.'

Now why did everything he said sound like an allusion to sex? Was that his intention? She refused to meet his eyes for longer than a distracting second. Instead, she fixed her gaze on a point midway down his chest. 'We open tomorrow,' she said agitatedly. 'And we're having a party. I even sent you an invitation. Didn't you get it?'

'Yeah. I got it a couple of days ago.' He had ripped open the envelope with its oddly familiar writing which seemed to have become more fluid over the years. And he had felt a mixture of different emotions as he'd pulled out the thick card within. Surprise that Donna had had the audacity to ask him—as well as a burning curiosity to see what she had done to the place. And if the reception area was anything to go by she was onto a winner.

'Were you surprised?' she queried. 'To be invited?'

'A little. I didn't think I'd be number one on your guest list—'

'You weren't,' she agreed calmly. 'More like number one hundred and one.'

'So why bother?'

'Because I suspected you'd probably gatecrash if I didn't! Or go to extraordinary lengths to disguise yourself as an ordinary punter just so you could have a look round. I thought I'd save you the trouble.'

'How very sweet of you.'

'Wasn't it?'

'And maybe because you wanted to show the place off?' he suggested. 'To put my nose out of joint by demonstrating how well you'd done?'

'Maybe there was a bit of that,' she agreed. 'You can't blame me for that, Marcus.'

'No,' he said slowly, looking around. 'I guess I can't.'

'So, are you be coming to the opening, or not?'

That slow, secret smile of hers made him ache in places it was uncomfortable to ache in public. 'I'll think about it.'

'It'll give you the perfect opportunity to see the place properly.'

'No, it won't,' he contradicted flatly. He had been having trouble sleeping over these past few days and he didn't like it. He didn't like it one bit. He glared at the unwitting cause of his sleeplessness.

'You'll have all the great and the good crowded in here, fawning over you like sycophants,' he said. 'You'll speak less than ten words to every person in the room, and you certainly won't be able to give anyone your undivided attention.' He paused. 'And I want your undivided attention, Donna.'

'Do you? And do you always get what you want?'

'Usually.' The light blue eyes hardened. 'Though not always, of course. Honesty is notoriously difficult to come by, isn't it? Especially when you're employing staff.'

'Oh!' she exclaimed sarcastically. 'Was that a pointed remark—directed at me?'

Marcus shrugged. 'Put it this way—I'd certainly have difficulty writing you a good reference.'

'Then it's a good thing I'm not asking you for one!' She realised that his boast of earlier had not been an idle one, and that he had no intention of going anywhere. So why fight it? 'Okay, Marcus,' she sighed. 'You win! Come with me and I'll show you around. What would you like to see first?'

He didn't miss a beat. 'Whatever you'd like to show me. I'm easy.'

'How about the kitchen?' she said brightly.

She could feel her heart bashing against her ribcage as he followed her along to the kitchen and cast a swift, professional eye over the fittings.

'Nice,' he commented, running the flat of his hand over a giant steel oven as if he were smoothing the flank of a horse. 'This is very nearly top of the range. Big investment.'

'It needs to be. I'm going to be doing lots of baking. Scones. Cakes. Meringues.'

He shot her a glance. 'You aren't planning to do all the cooking yourself?'

'Yes, that's right,' she shot back. 'Along with the cleaning, the ordering, the serving and the accounts! Don't be daft, Marcus—I'm going to have people working for me, of course.'

'How many?'

'Well, just a couple, to start with. A waitress—remember Sarah, who showed you in?'

'Vaguely.'

'And a woman called Ally Lawson, who's going to be helping me with the baking.'

Marcus frowned. 'How many covers do you have?'

'We can seat thirty inside, and another thirty in the garden—though obviously we'll only be able to use that when the weather's good enough.'

'Then you simply aren't going to have enough staff,' he told her.

She resented the advice, even though she knew he was right. 'I know that—I'm not completely stupid! I'm going to fill in wherever someone is needed—I can bake and wait tables myself. And I'm going to get some casual staff during the summer, when it gets really busy. There are plenty of students around who want jobs.' She swallowed down her desire to have him praise her, and gestured with her hand instead. 'Come through and see the tea-room.'

'The tea-room,' he echoed faintly, as she pushed the door open into a low room with a beamed ceiling.

Marcus thought that it was like stepping back in time—it had dark wood absolutely everywhere and he could smell furniture polish. Each table had a starched white tablecloth with a lace trim flouncing around the legs, and there were brightly polished copper kettles and old-fashioned jugs filled with bluebells.

Donna was proud of what she had achieved, and Marcus Foreman was respected in the business. His opinion was worth something. 'What do you think?'

He didn't need to. 'It's old-fashioned,' he told her bluntly.

'Well, of course it's old-fashioned—afternoon tea always *is*! People don't come to a city like Winchester and trawl round the ancient streets and gaze up at the cathedral and Jane Austen's house in wonder—and expect something high-tech afterwards! They don't want sushi or a three-bean salad! They want featherlight sponges on bone-china plates! Scones with thick cream and homemade jam—just like Mother used to make!'

His eyes narrowed with cruel perception. 'Why, is that what *your* mother used to make?'

Donna blushed, and hated herself for doing so, and thought that if she was a merciless kind of person she might have brought up the subject of *his* mother. 'You know very well she didn't!'

He shook his head. 'But that's where you're wrong, sugar—I don't. I know nothing at all. I thought that your mother was a noble, committed actress, because that's what you led me to believe.'

'With good reason. Seeing as how you set yourself up to pass judgement on everyone else!'

'I have to admit that it came as something of a shock to me,' he continued, as if she hadn't spoken, 'to discover that she used to strip down to a few strategically placed tassels and then gyrate her pelvis in men's faces!'

'And you w-wonder why I never told you?' she demanded shakily. 'Because you haven't got the imagination to see that it was the only option for her! She was a single mother!'

'Not the only option, Donna,' he grated. 'Thousands of women who are single mothers don't become strippers! There are plenty of other jobs available.'

'I'm not ashamed of my mother, or what she did!' she said proudly. 'And whatever *you* say won't make me! However it may have seemed from the outside—*I* know the truth! She may have been misdirected—but she wasn't promiscuous.' She took a deep, shuddering breath.

'She wasn't really interested in men—she was hurt

too badly when my father left. I certainly didn't grow up knowing a series of "uncles". She kept her morals, and she didn't just fritter her money away like so many of her colleagues did. She saved, and set herself up in business on the proceeds—'

'That's the bed and breakfast place you were once so scornful of?'

'Yes!' she snapped. 'And that was because I was of an age where I didn't appreciate all her hard work and sacrifice—so of course I was scornful!' And she'd been desperately trying to hide the truth from him. 'But my mother made a success of her B&B. She worked hard!'

He saw her blinking rather rapidly and felt an intrusive pang of conscience. He found that he wanted to draw her into the circle of his arms and stroke that gleaming, fiery hair. He glanced down at a menu instead. 'And what is she doing now?'

'She's dead. She died two and a half years ago. The money from her business helped me buy this place.'

'Donna, I'm—'

'No, you're not!' she told him fiercely. 'Don't say you're sorry, Marcus—because you're not!'

'Listen to me,' he told her, and his voice was just as insistent. 'Of course I'm sorry that she's dead! I lost my own mother when I was a child. I know how badly it hurts—whatever age you are.'

When he spoke like that—in that soft, urgent way, as if the words came straight from the heart—*that* was when he was at his most dangerous, Donna realised. And the danger lay in thinking that he saw her as his equal. And he didn't. He never had.

But he would.

'Well, thank you for that,' she said stiffly.

'Don't sound so surprised. I'm not a complete bad guy.'

'You just do a very convincing imitation, is that it?'

He laughed, and found that he badly wanted to kiss her. And it was a long time since he had wanted to *kiss* a woman.

Donna looked at him, her courage deserting her as she realised that he still had the power to make her want him. Very badly. Had he taken an exam in how to move, she wondered distractedly, so that a woman would get turned on just by watching him?

He was resting his jeaned bottom against one of the tables, his long legs stretching out in front of him, making the table look like a flimsy little stick of dolls' house furniture. And why was he looking at her like that? As if he'd like to eat her up for breakfast.

He met her eyes. She looked so cool and so untouchable and so damned *superior*. 'I notice that you still haven't asked me anything about my baby brother,' he observed. 'Surprising, really—I thought that you and Lucas were the best of buddies.'

'He always found time to talk to me, if that's what you mean.' She wiped her finger along a gleaming surface, delighted to see it come away dust-free. 'How is he?'

He gave a grim smile. 'Isn't it odd that the two of you didn't stay in touch? After all, what Lucas didn't know about you wasn't really worth knowing, was it, Donna? Such a very *intimate* friendship—'

'I was never intimate with your brother!'

'Of course you were,' he scorned softly. 'You shared thoughts. Secrets. You don't have to rip all your clothes off and have sex with someone in order to be intimate, you know!'

She was unprepared for her own soft venom, but maybe it had been silently building up inside since that long-ago night when his virile body had terrified the life out of her and his face had been that of a wild, dark stranger. 'I'm surprised that intimacy is a topic you want to touch on, Marcus.'

Their eyes met.

'Ouch,' he winced softly. 'Be careful, now. If you're going to accuse a man of being a disaster in bed you're going to hit him where he hurts hardest.'

'What, dent his pride, you mean? Or his ego?'

'I was thinking of somewhere a lot more basic than that, sugar,' he taunted, revelling in the fact that by now her cheeks were as hot and as flushed as if she'd just run up a steep hill. 'Challenge a man like that and he's going to respond in one way only. By demanding a repeat performance. What do you say to that, Donna? Shall we let history repeat itself and hope that the outcome is more mutually satisfactory this time?'

Donna froze. Her mouth felt as dry as unbuttered toast. She ignored the question, and all its implications—though she wondered if she would have been able to if he had put his arms around her, instead of discussing it in that cold, clinical way. 'I thought we were talking about Lucas.'

'Ah, yes. Lucas.'

His mouth relaxed into a smile which surprised her—a proud, elder brother kind of smile.

'Well, Lucas seems to have made good—confounding all predictions to the contrary. He took his camera round the world with him and got as far as South America, where—rather amazingly—he fell in love.'

'What's so amazing about that?'

'Well, he'd never managed to stay faithful to a woman

before.' He searched her expression for disappointment, but if there was any then she was hiding it well. 'He married Rosa and is now the proud father of twin boys. He runs a moderately successful studio in Caracas—taking wedding and christening photos and studio portraits. And he seems very contented.'

'Good heavens!' said Donna faintly.

'Heartbroken?'

'Don't be silly. I just can't imagine Lucas as a husband—let alone as a *father*! He always seemed too restless to ever be described as contented.'

'That's what the love of a good woman does for you.' He paused. 'Pity you didn't qualify.'

'I never wanted your brother—'

'But he wanted you.'

'Maybe he did. But that was nothing to do with me. He knew I wasn't interested in him—not in that way.'

He shook his head. 'You played us off against one another, Donna. You know you did. I was the lucky recipient of all those smouldering looks you used to send out—but it was Lucas who was treated to all the cosy little chats, wasn't it?'

Donna frowned in confusion. He made it sound as if he had been excluded. 'But you didn't want that kind of relationship,' she protested. 'Not with me, anyway. You held me at arm's length, Marcus—you know you did. You used to clam up if anything remotely *personal* ever reared its ugly head. You were so busy being the boss. Keeping your distance.'

'Just not very effectively,' he observed, and his voice sounded bitter. 'Well, not in your case.' He shook his head as the memory buzzed like a persistent fly. 'I thought you were sexually experienced, Donna—I really did. When I discovered you were a virgin I couldn't believe it! I was astonished—'

'But not pleased?'

'No,' he said bluntly.

It still hurt more than it had a right to. 'I thought that it was every man's fantasy. To be the first lover.'

'Not this man.'

She didn't stop to ask him why because she had a good idea what he might say. Virgins were girls who had grown up in dinky houses with fitted carpets. The kind of girl that men ended up marrying. Not the kind of girl they wanted a quick fling with.

She stared at him, dazzled by the beauty of his eyes as their ice-blue light washed over her face. 'So what do you want, Marcus?' she demanded. 'Why have you come here today?'

He narrowed his eyes assessingly. Didn't she know? Couldn't she tell? That he wanted to eradicate all those memories of that night and to replace them with something which would make her ache with longing.

And the way he was behaving towards her—he wouldn't even make it past first base.

'What happened to all your freckles?' he asked suddenly, leaning fractionally forward so that her flesh radiated its warmth towards him.

It was such an abrupt change of mood and subject that Donna screwed her eyes up at him. 'Freckles?' she repeated suspiciously.

'Those tiny brown marks sprinkled all over your face,' he teased. 'You used to have more—your skin was covered in them. Remember?'

'I started staying out of the sun,' she answered.

'And you lost them along the way, with the frizzy hair and the dungarees?'

It should have sounded like a slur, but when he said it in that oddly indulgent way it was very nearly a compliment. Suddenly Donna felt more than nervous. When he was being nice to her, like this, she was just a hair's breadth away from feeling as vulnerable as she'd ever been in his company.

'My hair is still frizzy when it's untied,' she told him repressively. 'And I still wear dungarees when I'm not working.'

'Do you?' He was silent for a moment as he stared down into her smooth, pale face and was filled with a nostalgic desire to see her looking the way she used to. With those big, fat ginger plaits and the freckle-spattered face and her oddly secretive smile.

Unthinkingly, he allowed the tip of his tongue to slick the corners of his mouth, and found her following the movement with eyes which managed to be both fascinated and disapproving.

'Licking your lips?' she observed. 'Don't you get fed properly?'

'Why, are you offering?'

'I've got quite enough catering to be going on with,' she answered coolly. 'Now, I really think it's time you were going, Marcus—you've seen just about everything there is to see.'

'Not the garden,' he objected.

'You'll get your opportunity to see that tomorrow.' She met his eyes. 'If you're planning on coming?'

He fought against his better judgement, and lost. 'I wouldn't miss it for the world,' he murmured.

CHAPTER FIVE

'DONNA—you've worked miracles!'

Donna smiled politely at the Mayor's wife, who had worked something of a miracle herself, she thought. The miracle being how she managed to remain standing after eating three rounds of smoked salmon sandwiches, four scones with cream and jam and an enormous wedge of coffee and walnut cake!

'Why, thank you, Mrs Armstrong! Can I fetch you another cup of tea?'

'Oh, would you, dear? That last piece of cake has made me terribly thirsty.'

'I'll go and get it,' said Donna. She made her way through the tea-room, smiling at people on the way, noting with satisfaction that every single table was full. Just by the kitchen door she passed Ally, who was pushing her way out, bearing a tray loaded with vanilla butterfly cakes and slices of lemon madeira.

'What do you reckon?' whispered Donna. 'Do we have a success on our hands?'

'We most certainly do! I'd even do a thumbs-up if I didn't have my hands full!' laughed Ally. 'You can sit back and rest on your laurels once they've all gone!'

'They don't really show much sign of going, do they?' said Donna.

'Not really. Though I suppose we shouldn't complain. Most restaurateurs complain about the trouble they have getting people *in*—not getting them out! I'd better go and feed the hungry masses. I'll see you later,' said Ally.

In the kitchen, Sarah was busy putting scones onto a beautiful bone-china plate. She saw Donna and turned her eyes up to heaven. 'Just how many did you invite, for heaven's sake? Did no one at all turn you down?'

'Oh, just a couple,' said Donna lightly. 'No one important.' She had tried to tell herself that she wasn't disappointed. So *what* if Marcus hadn't shown?

So why did she keep looking up every time the bell rang on the front door? Only to have to force a smile when she saw that it wasn't who she'd thought it might be.

But the afternoon had been a huge success.

As well as the Mayor, they had managed to get their local Member of Parliament to squeeze a brief cup of Lapsang Suchong into his busy schedule. The press had arrived early, and stayed longer than expected, especially when Donna had produced a wine cask from the fridge because they'd all claimed that they didn't want to drink tea.

A female journalist's eyes had lit up briefly as her antennae tested whether there was a story. 'Are you allowed to serve alcohol here?' she had asked doubtfully.

'Oh, yes—I've got my drinks licence,' Donna had said proudly. 'During the winter I'm going to serve mulled wine and mince pies.'

'Yum!' the journalist had said.

After a good deal of discussion Donna, Ally and Sarah had all worn shiny black short-sleeved dresses which came to the knee, with cute little white muslin aprons over the top. And they had all been convulsed with the giggles while trying them on.

'These are our "special occasion" dresses!' announced Donna. 'For high days and holidays!'

'Donna, I can't wear this!' Sarah had protested. 'I look like every man's fantasy of a French maid!'

'Only if your skirt were half that length—with lacy-topped stockings showing,' Donna had argued. 'Anyway—there's no law written down that says that waitresses have to wear unflattering clothes. You both look absolutely gorgeous, if you must know!'

'Well, so do you,' Ally had said, with a wink.

When everyone had gone home at last, they cleared the tables, put all the clean glass and china away and swept the kitchen floor. Then the three women flopped down at a table and congratulated themselves on the efficient service they had provided.

'Wasn't that man supposed to be coming?' asked Sarah.

'Man?' Ally did a mock double-take. 'Did I hear you mention a *man*?'

Donna liked Ally, and had been glad to give her the job. She was thirty-three, attractive and blonde. And separated. Her husband had left her—saying that he wanted to spend his life with a woman he had met in a hotel bar. He had told Ally that he was 'sorry' for the disruption he was causing, and what he'd said to Charlotte—their five-year-old daughter—was anyone's guess. So far, according to Ally, she was unable to speak of her father without bursting into noisy tears.

'Which man are we talking about?' persisted Ally, looking round the empty tea-room as if a member of the opposite sex might suddenly materialise.

'Donna's friend,' said Sarah. 'The tall, good-looking one with the dark hair. But he's not here.'

'He's not my friend,' protested Donna. 'I don't even like him.'

'Oh, don't you?' said Sarah, clearly not believing a

word of it. 'So why did you show him round the place yesterday, looking all pink and excited and hot underneath the collar?'

Donna sighed. 'Because I used to work for him. And I *wasn't* pink-faced and excited.'

'Er, *right*,' said Ally, screwing her face up in confusion. 'Has he got a name?'

'Yes, it's Foreman,' said Donna reluctantly, knowing that Ally was a local girl and wondering if she had heard of him.

Ally's eyes widened. She clearly had.

'Not Marcus Foreman?'

'That's the one.'

'Mmm! What's he like?'

Donna hesitated. 'He's—'

'He's standing right over there,' said Sarah, from out of the corner of her mouth.

Donna looked up to see Marcus framed on the threshold of the doorway, a shaft of sunshine gilding the edges of his hair so that he resembled a dark, gleaming angel.

Their eyes connected and then he smiled, and something extraordinary happened to Donna as he began walking towards her. It was like a blurred picture coming into focus. Like coming inside from the bitter cold. The world and her place in it suddenly made sense. Her resistance flew and she stared up at him, feeling as punch-drunk as a boxer.

'Hello, Marcus,' she said weakly.

'Hello, Donna. How did it go?'

'If you'd been here when you should have been you would have found out for yourself.'

He found the rebuke stimulating. But right then he found everything about her stimulating. Especially in that outrageously sexy black dress, with the pure white apron over the top. 'You said you were going to show me the garden, remember?' He gave a crinkly smile at the other two women. 'But maybe you'd better introduce me first.'

Sarah's facial muscles went into a kind of spasm as she gazed up at him.

Donna almost smiled. It would be funny if it wasn't so predictable. 'Sarah Flowers. Ally Lawson. This is Marcus Foreman.'

Sarah and Ally both leapt to their feet as if the movement had been scripted.

'I've been past your hotel millions of times!' babbled Sarah. 'But of course I've never eaten there.'

'Why not?' he asked.

Ally came to Sarah's rescue. 'It's a wee bit too expensive,' she said bluntly.

Marcus smiled. 'People usually find that it's far less expensive than they imagine—in fact it's comparable to plenty of other restaurants with lower ratings. Tell you what,' he added thoughtfully, 'if each of you want to bring a partner—say on a Monday or Tuesday evening, when we're quiet—you can eat there on me!'

'Gosh, thanks!' beamed Sarah.

'Yes, thanks very much!' echoed Ally.

They left soon after, and Donna stood and waved them off down the street, where the cherry blossom was being rained down in a pale pink storm by a suddenly blustery April wind.

She locked the door behind them and went back into the tea-room to find that Marcus hadn't moved, and her heart lurched with a fierce kind of excitement at the way he was staring at her.

'That was very kind of you,' she said unsteadily. 'To offer Ally and Sarah a free meal.'

He raised his eyebrows. 'Don't sound so surprised.'

'I'm not, actually. You like playing the role of bene-factor—you did it to me, remember?'

He bit back his automatic reply to *that* unwittingly provocative remark. 'You have the ability to make an act of kindness sound like a character defect, Donna.'

'Do I? I'm sorry.' She didn't know whether to sit or stand. She felt uncomfortable, too aware of herself. And him.

'You still haven't told me how your opening went.'

'I know I haven't.' She looked him straight in the eye. 'But that's not why you're here, is it? If you were interested in the fortunes of my tea-room you would have turned up on time like everyone else and seen for yourself. Wouldn't you?'

His smile was rueful. 'I guess I would.'

'So what, then?'

'You want the truth?'

She nodded.

'You don't need me to tell you, Donna. You know yourself.' His eyes had never been bluer. 'I want to make love to you.'

Her mouth fell open. *'Marcus!'*

He shook his head. 'You should never have come back if you didn't want this to happen,' he told her softly, and his words were like a sweet caress on her skin. 'Nine years ago we blew everything—and I want the chance to put it right.'

'Oh. I see.' Her heart plummeted with disappointment. But then what had she been expecting—a declaration of undying love? 'Was I the one lover who didn't give you full marks for performance? Is that what this is all about?'

'No. It's about getting rid of a desire that isn't going

to go away. Look me in the eye, Donna, and tell me truthfully that you don't want me just as badly. Do that and I'll go away and leave you alone.'

She couldn't.

If only he would play the game. Tell her that he'd never stopped thinking about her, that he couldn't go on living without her. But he was an honest man. She knew that. Everything in his world was black and white. 'Don't do this to me, Marcus,' she whispered. 'Please. I can't fight you.'

'I don't want you to fight me,' he whispered back. 'I want you to give in to what you really want to do.'

His voice moved over her senses and she shook her head distractedly.

The movement made his eyes darken, and unexpectedly he reached up and touched her hair and the gesture took her completely off her guard. 'Amazing,' he murmured. 'I've never met another woman with hair like yours, Donna. Like fire. Rich and raw and hot.' He was conscious of echoing words he had spoken to her once before, as if he wanted to re-run the film and change the ending. 'Why don't you kiss me, huh? Come on, sugar. Kiss me.'

Over the years she had erected a wall around her heart, and Marcus was demolishing it, brick by brick, exposing the emotional wasteland which lay beneath. She jerked her head back with an effort. 'We shouldn't be doing this.'

'I don't agree, and neither do you, not really. I can read it in your eyes. And your body.' His eyes flickered over the black satin dress that made the curves of her body so luscious and irresistible. He could see the swell of her breasts as they strained against the material, their rock-hard tips pushing towards him, and he thought he might pass out with longing. 'See for yourself if you don't believe me.'

Donna glanced down at her swollen breasts, her fingers flying protectively to her throat, and she looked down in horror to discover that her hand was shaking uncontrollably.

And he saw, too. Saw and smiled. 'Yes,' he said slowly. 'Yes, I thought so.' His gaze licked over her like warm syrup as he took her trembling hand in his, locking their fingers together and guiding them to lie over the muffled thundering of his heart. 'Can you feel that?'

Her lips seemed glued together. She wasn't able to answer him. Or look at him. All she could do was feel the pumping of his life-blood beneath her fingertips.

She lifted her gaze to his, her eyes full of question and need, and her breath escaped in a gentle sound as she saw the desire which had darkened his eyes.

'Kiss me, Donna,' he urged again. 'You know you want to.'

She trembled. 'S-sometimes I want to eat more ice-cream than I should—doesn't mean I'm going to do it.'

Without any warning, he brought his mouth crushing down on hers. The last time he had kissed her she had felt like a gawky novice in his arms. She had been too overwhelmed by him not to feel terrible, debilitating nerves. But not this time.

She opened her lips and shuddered, lost in the erotic power of his kiss. 'That...wasn't fair!' she gasped.

'Maybe not, but it was good, wasn't it?' he murmured. 'I know what you want, don't I? Maybe I always did. Just back then I was too selfish. And I'm going to make it up to you.'

He brought the palms of his hands around her back and down her spine until they cupped her satin-covered bottom to bring her into the cradle of his hips, and she whimpered as she felt him rock against her. 'This time I'm going to take it slow.'

'Marcus...' Was that hot, jerky little voice really hers?

He was kissing her neck, the curve of her jaw. 'I'm going to have you calling my name out loud,' he said indistinctly. 'I'm going to give you so much pleasure that you'll be begging me to stop!'

She couldn't believe that he was saying these things to her, and she couldn't believe how much it was turning her on, bringing her to a fever-pitch of excitement that made her gasp something that was muffled and indistinct.

He lifted his head, his eyes glazed. 'What is it?'

'I don't *know,*' she almost wept.

He began to lift up the satin skirt of her dress. The air was like a cool whisper on her thighs and she felt the pooling of unbearable need as she swayed against him.

He looked down at her. 'Want to go somewhere else?'

She wanted... 'I want—'

'Tell me, sugar. Tell me what it is you want.'

'You *know*!' she gasped. Nine years she had waited to have him do this to her again. Only this time she wasn't going to ruin it with her naive hopes and expectations. 'You know damned well!'

He lifted his head from her neck to look at her flushed face and his smile was triumphant and heartbreakingly predatory. Oh, yes, he knew all right.

Hell, much more of feeling her breasts jutting tantalisingly into his chest like that and he... But just imagine if a passing tourist should glance in through the window and see them. Think what *that* would do for his reputation!

Or hers.

He drew a deep breath to clip an urgent sentence out. 'Where's your bedroom?'

Somewhere, even in the hot mists of unstoppable desire, Donna heard warning bells. No, not there. A room where he would be surrounded by all *her* things. Because that was where it had all gone wrong last time, when he had been the big, virile lover and she the foolish, frightened virgin. She didn't want Marcus cramped this time, or daunted by her narrow bed and the starched and frilly white linen she had accumulated over the years. Her room was too feminine for a man like Marcus. He would have no place there.

She shook her head. 'Not my bedroom.'

For one horrific and unimaginable moment he really thought she was going to kick him out, and he could barely get his next words out. 'Where, then?'

'Upstairs.'

'Want to take me there?'

'O-okay.'

'I'm half tempted to carry you,' he growled as he saw her move with the gawky uncertainty of a newborn foal.

'No, don't. You couldn't.'

'Want to bet?' He could hardly believe what he was doing as he took her by the hand and swung her easily over his shoulder in a fireman's lift to carry her up the stairs. What was happening to him? Since when had he decided to play masterful?

He was careful to keep his eyes averted from the obvious distractions of her bottom—otherwise he suspected he might go tumbling back down the way he had come. And in a way he was glad to have the physical diversion of carrying her. It took the edge off his passion, and maybe that was what he needed where she was concerned. For there must be no repeat of last time...

'Just here,' whispered Donna.

He pushed open the door with his knee and set her down, barely noticing the fittings or the decor—just that the bed was huge, thank God. He turned to the woman by his side, her eyes huge and dark and green in a face tight-white with expectation.

He bent his head and negligently brushed his lips against hers. 'Now,' he said indistinctly, 'where were we?'

'I don't remember,' she gasped.

He kissed her until her knees grew weak, and then began to unbutton the tiny satin-covered buttons which ran down the entire length of her dress, but his fingers were trembling and the aching in his groin was unbearable. He couldn't believe that this was happening to him again. He felt powerless—as if some great, ungovernable force was controlling him. He lifted his mouth away from hers. 'Can you do this?' he beseeched.

Her fingers were only marginally less shaky than his, but she guessed it was easier to take off your own clothes than someone else's, and soon the dress had been slung in a far corner of the bedroom.

And Marcus was down to a T-shirt and a pair of black silk boxer shorts.

Donna swallowed and stared at him, unable to tear her eyes away.

He pulled his T-shirt off in a single movement and saw her hand reach round to her back to unclip her bra. He let his eyes drink in the creamy flesh which spilled over the confining black lace.

'No, don't. Leave it on!' he said unsteadily. 'And

come here.' He pulled back the cover and climbed into bed, holding his arms out to her, and she went into them like a child going home, almost falling on top of him in her eagerness to be enfolded in that warm embrace.

'Oh, Donna,' he said softly, and ran his fingertips around the oval curve of her jaw. 'You little beauty.'

She could feel muscle and bone through the warm satin of his skin, and the hot, hard throb of desire nudging against her. 'I can't believe I'm here, like this. Doing this,' she stumbled. 'With you. I told myself I never would, no matter what the provocation.'

He tipped up her chin so that she couldn't escape his penetrating stare. 'For God's sake, Donna—if you don't want to go through with it then tell me—but tell me now!'

She shook her head. 'You know I couldn't let you go, even if I wanted to.' Her lashes fluttered down to partially conceal her eyes. 'And I don't,' she added huskily.

He gave a moan as he pulled her over him, moving her up the bed so that he could unclip her bra, and her breasts came tumbling out, one falling with sweet accuracy into his mouth.

'Mmm. Bullseye!' he murmured, and Donna actually giggled.

'That's better,' he said approvingly.

He suckled her while she moaned and wriggled against him until he thought he would explode with need like a champagne cork.

'Slide my shorts off,' he whispered, and his fingers flicked tantalisingly at her panties as she did so, the tips coming away moist and fragrant with her musky, feminine scent. He placed his middle finger in her mouth, their eyes locking helplessly as she sucked on it.

'Oh, God,' she whimpered.

'Do you like that?'

'*Yes!*' she almost sobbed.

'Want to make love?'

'*Yes!*'

He felt her reaching to find him, exquisitely encircling him as she had once done as an untutored girl. And it was with a feeling of *déjà vu* that something nudged insistently at his memory. 'Are you on the pill these days?'

Her reply was nearly, Of course not—except that there was no 'of course' about it.

And there was no reason in the world for her to be offended by what was, in fact, a very sensible question. Especially under the circumstances. Why wouldn't he think she was on the pill? Most women of her age were. 'No. No, I'm not.'

He swore softly as his hand groped down to find his jeans and fumbled around until he had fished a packet of condoms out of the back pocket.

He slid the protection on with both regret and relief, part of him wanting no barrier between them. But only a foolish, inconsequential part. And that was when he stopped thinking and started feeling as he thrust long and hard and drove deep into her hot, welcoming flesh.

When Donna opened her eyes it had grown dark, and she blinked once or twice, wondering why she was sleeping in the guest bedroom and what exactly had woken her.

Until a slight movement set off the first trigger of recollection and memory washed over her bare skin like a warm bath. She became aware that her breasts were tingling, their tips still prickling with sweet sensation, aware too of an aching deep inside her. As if she had been using muscles she had never used before. Maybe she had. She smiled as she reached out to click the lamp on, and the room was flooded with light.

Stretching lazily, she turned her head to see Marcus pulling on his jeans, the look on his face changing from one of dark and flushed contentment to a closed and wary expression when he saw her watching him.

'Hi,' he said.

She might have hoped for something a little less non-committal, in view of what they had been doing over the last few hours.

Still. Just because they had both enjoyed the best sex ever, that didn't mean he was about to start telling her he loved her! That would just be a bonus, she thought rather wistfully.

'Hi,' she said, and smiled as she sat up, her hair half-in and half-out of the French plait, and strands of it falling over her freckled shoulders.

Marcus averted his eyes from the spectacular movement of her breasts, but it was too late to stop his body responding. He bent down to try and locate his watch and hoped that she hadn't noticed.

He still felt shaken by what had just happened. He had made love to her over and over again—more times than he had ever done to a woman before. But he had been unprepared for the power of their lovemaking. He had experienced blissful abandonment, yes—but it had overwhelmed him in a way that was completely alien to him. And he wasn't sure that he liked it.

'I didn't want to wake you,' he said, as he hunted around for his shoe.

'Was that why you were creeping around like a thief?'

He found the shoe and slipped it on, then buckled up

his wristwatch. 'Actually, you looked so peaceful lying there that I thought I'd leave you.'

Donna sighed. She wasn't going to clutch onto his ankles to prevent him from leaving the room, but neither was she going to act as if they had spent the afternoon talking about the state of the economy! 'And of course the advantage of leaving me to sleep is that you could avoid having to answer any awkward questions.'

He went very still. 'You make it sound like I'm on trial.'

'Not really. I just wondered what the hurry was, that's all. I mean, I presume you haven't got somebody else to rush back to?'

'Shouldn't you have asked that *before* we went to bed?' he drawled.

Like the stereotype of a possessive girlfriend, she heard herself saying, 'Is that a yes or a no?'

His mouth thinned. 'I only ever sleep with one woman at a time.'

That hurt. And so did the dismissive way he spoke, which meant that Donna couldn't pretend any longer even if she'd wanted to. And suddenly she didn't want to. She wasn't a little girl who couldn't face knowing the truth—however much it hurt.

'You know, I'm getting the distinct impression that we have just made our second big mistake, Marcus.'

He tugged the T-shirt down and tucked it into the waistband of his jeans. 'Mistake?' he queried, looking faintly surprised, as if this were perfectly normal behaviour and she was breaking some unspoken code of conduct. 'Oh, Donna, please don't let us go down that route! Nobody had to drag you to bed. Not this time—nor the time before. You were the one who came back to Winchester. You were the one who walked into my restaurant giving me the green light. What did you expect? You must have known that something like this would happen.'

The green light? She kept her voice calm—though heaven only knew how. 'Okay, maybe I'm overreacting. So why the long face and the keep-away body language? And why now—after what just happened. It was good, wasn't it?'

'It was bloody fantastic,' he said softly. 'You know it was.'

'Well, then?'

Marcus screwed his eyes up, as though a light were blinding them. He seemed to choose his words carefully. 'I don't like what you make me become.'

'And what's that?'

His voice deepened. 'You saw for yourself. You don't need me to tell you.'

Donna nodded. She had been stunned by the depth of his passion, at the way he had stripped away layer upon layer of himself—to reveal a tantalising glimpse of what lay at the very core of the man. The free spirit which had been obscured by the burden of responsibility. Surely he had the courage to face up to the truth?

'You mean you're worried that you'll end up like your mother?'

There was a long, fraught silence. 'What do you know about my mother?' he asked icily.

'Lots.'

The blue eyes looked frozen. 'How?'

'Lucas told me.'

'Oh, did he? And what exactly did he say?'

'That she was beautiful. And wild. And that she was unfaithful to your father—time and time again. He said that the rows which resulted were so bad you both had to be sent away to school, but that he couldn't bear to divorce her.'

'And did he say anything else?' he asked, in a deceptively silky voice.

Donna shrugged. 'He said that she was out of control.' She met his furious gaze with a candid stare. 'And that's how you were today, wasn't it, Marcus? Out of control.'

Tense seconds ticked by. 'Your comments aren't just intrusive—they're inaccurate. Passion has nothing to do with fidelity. And fidelity is a matter of personal choice.'

'Marcus—'

'As amateur psychologists I'm afraid you and Lucas leave a lot to be desired,' he continued, and his mouth hardened. 'Don't tell me that you were spinning fantasies, Donna. Expecting to hear me say that you're the one and only just because we had an afternoon of great sex?'

'Of course I wasn't.' Donna pulled the bedspread up to cover her bare breasts.

'The debt I owed you has been cancelled,' he added softly. 'So we're quits now.'

She could scarcely get the words out. 'You mean…you've redeemed yourself—sexually—by giving me the orgasms I missed out on before?'

His look of outrage was worth what it had cost her to reduce their afternoon to simple mechanics.

'I wouldn't have put it quite like that.'

'Oh? How would you have put it, then? Dressed it up with a euphemism? The earth moved! The bell rang!'

'Don't spoil what just happened!' he snapped. 'Just face up to the truth, the same way that I have had to. There's too much history between us, Donna. Too much water has flowed underneath the bridge—not just a gentle stream in our case, more like a bloody great torrent!'

She returned his mocking glance with a face devoid of expression. And why was she cowering beneath the bedclothes as if she was still the humble chambermaid and he was still her lord and master?

She slid her long legs over the side of the bed and heard his gasp as the covers fell away and she stood up like Venus rising out of the waves.

He swallowed. 'What are you doing?'

'I'm going to fetch my clothes from next door. So that I can see you out. There's no crime against that, is there?'

Marcus stood there, open-mouthed. In the heat of passion his vision had been limited to whichever particular area had been given his undivided attention. Seen in isolation, each breast was utterly magnificent, the indentation of her waist just perfect and the swell of her bottom every man's most torrid fantasy.

But put them together and you had sheer perfection.

A comment that Lucas had once made came drifting back over the years. 'You can see why her mother was a stripper!' And the blatantly sexy compliment toughened his resolve.

'I can see myself out.'

Donna's eyes hardened. 'What's the matter? Ashamed to be seen leaving in case anyone knows what you've been up to? Well, don't worry, Marcus—people can't tell you've had sex just by looking at you, you know! Besides, I want to lock up behind you.' And she wiggled out of the room to find some clothes.

He waited, feeling more het-up and confused than he could ever remember. She was nothing but a manipulating little witch! Why had she waited until he was dressed and ready to leave before flaunting her body at him like that?

When Donna reappeared she had redone her French plait and put on a pair of jeans and an old plaid shirt.

Marcus should have felt less agitated, but he didn't. Suddenly she looked so scrubbed and *wholesome*. Funny how that could be just as erotic as satin and lace.

'Let's go,' she said coldly, and she led the way downstairs.

They didn't say a word to one another as he followed her towards the front door, and the loud ringing of the doorbell made them both start.

Now who the hell was *that*? wondered Donna, and she pulled open the door to find Tony Paxman standing on the doorstep, a foolish grin on his face and a bottle of champagne in his hand.

Marcus felt mad jealousy rip through him as the good-looking lawyer handed her the wine and gave a helpless kind of smile.

'Hi, Donna. Sorry I'm late—I had to go to court with a client. This is for you.' He nodded cautiously. 'Hi, Marcus.'

Marcus gave a grim nod.

'Oh, how thoughtful of you, Tony!' enthused Donna, overplaying her gratitude like mad. 'Come in!'

Tony looked at Marcus. 'Oh, but you're—'

'No, I'm not! Marcus is just leaving—aren't you, Marcus? Come and have a drink with me, Tony—I feel like celebrating! Have a wander round while I'm seeing Marcus out.'

The lawyer stepped inside, and Donna almost recoiled from the black, baleful look that Marcus sent searing in her direction.

'Goodbye,' she said quietly.

'Goodbye, Donna.' His glance was unfathomable as he watched Tony Paxman disappearing down the hallway. Then he looked into her eyes. 'A word of advice,' he said softly.

If she had known what was coming she would never have asked him. 'What?'

'Just don't forget to change the sheets first, huh?'

There was a short, breathless pause. She wanted to scream, but she didn't want to make a scene.

Instead, she shut the door firmly in his face.

CHAPTER SIX

TEMPERAMENTAL April drifted into glorious, golden May.

Donna went to an auction and bought a job lot of neglected garden furniture. She spent every evening rubbing it down and painting it all dark green, then she dotted the restored tables and chairs out onto the newly mown lawn.

They looked perfect in her own secret garden, where the spreading branches of the apple trees were bursting into tiny pink and white blossoms. Soon they would be able to start serving tea outside regularly—at the moment it was on sunny days only.

And business was booming. It seemed that Winchester had been crying out for a good, old-fashioned tea-room, because the public had greeted its arrival like an old friend. Every day they were full.

It appealed to people right across the board. The older generation approved because they could remember when afternoon tea had been a regular feature on the culinary calendar. The younger people liked it because they wished it still *was* taken regularly—or so they told Donna. It was popular with courting couples too, because tea was essentially a romantic meal, where people could linger unbothered over the scones. And tourists adored it because it fitted in with their perception of what traditional England was really like.

The days were long and busy, with Donna getting up at the crack of dawn to start making cakes and scones.

She enjoyed the warmth and smell of the baking, and
the sound of the radio playing and the birds singing outside. The Buttress had become her haven. After a long
time searching, she felt she had at last come home.

In fact, there was only one faint cloud on her horizon,
and that was Marcus—or, more accurately, what had
happened with Marcus upstairs in the guest bedroom.
But as the days blurred by even that became understand-
able. Acceptable, even. She was determined to be mod-
ern and mature about the experience. To remember the
good bits and blot out the bad.

As a relationship it was a non-starter, but she could
accept that. Of course she could. In fact, she couldn't
think of a single other woman of her acquaintance who
had not had something similar happen to her.

She had wondered how she would cope if she kept
bumping into him, but she did not bump into him. Not
once.

She saw him a couple of times from a safe distance,
and once when they were both shopping at Winchester's
open-air market. She felt an almost savage jolt of recognition as she spotted his tall, dark figure across the
square, and she could have *sworn* that he'd seen her. But
he didn't come over. Just walked resolutely on.

She realised what insular lives they led. Marcus had
his own little world and she had hers. They lived on
opposite sides of the same street, but they might have
lived on opposite sides of the world for all that their
lives collided.

It was towards the end of May that the first niggling
little doubt began to bother her in her quieter moments.

She made excuses.

She had been busy/stressed/worried. She had changed
jobs/changed area/changed home. But then a couple of

days became a couple of weeks, and her anxiety levels shot up—until she convinced herself that there was nothing to worry about.

Lots of women were late—and it wasn't as though she could be pregnant, was it? Donna felt her cheeks burning as she remembered how Marcus had sworn and insisted on wearing a condom. Every time. He had been determined that she shouldn't get pregnant.

No, her lateness was obviously psychological in origin.

She kept telling herself the same thing over and over again, even after May had slipped into June. But when she saw the 'July' written in black and white on the calendar she knew that she had to snap out of her denial mode and see whether her worst fears were about to be realised.

She drove to an out-of-town pharmacy and bought a pregnancy testing kit, and the following morning the blue indicator line in the test-tube told her that, yes, the worst-case scenario had actually happened.

She was pregnant.

Pregnant and alone and frightened. Knowing that she ought to tell someone, and knowing who the someone should be, and unable to face doing it.

She went to see her doctor, who destroyed her last remaining fantasy that maybe the result of the test had been false.

'Yes, you're pregnant.' She smiled. 'And you're a fit and healthy young woman—I can't see there being any problems. Congratulations!' she added, but Donna's lack of response made her frown. 'I *do* take it that congratulations are in order?'

Something primitive and protective stirred deep

within Donna's belly and consigned her doubts to history. 'Yes,' she said. 'They are. Thank you.'

'And the father?' asked Dr Baxter delicately. 'Is he around?'

'Er, not exactly.'

'Well, is he going to be supporting you?'

'I don't know,' said Donna simply. 'I haven't told him yet.'

She was longing to confide in someone. Ally, perhaps—who was a single mother herself. Or Sarah. But the troublesome voice of her conscience knew that she could not talk to them before she had talked to the one person she did not want to talk to.

She put it off and put it off, burying her head in the sand, as if by telling no one it would make it seem as if it wasn't real.

Except that it was real. The tingling weight of her newly aching breasts was real enough. As was the nausea, which seemed to be entirely random in when it hit her. One week she felt sick in the morning, the next her evenings were spent hovering within easy reach of a basin.

She put off telling anyone until one of her regular check-ups, when Dr Baxter beamed at her and said, 'Well, well, Donna. You've started showing at last, haven't you?'

'Sh-showing?'

Dr Baxter sent her a rather odd look and her voice was very gentle. 'That's right.' She smoothed her hand over the barely noticeable curve. 'It *is* usual in these circumstances for a woman to start looking as though she's going to have a baby, you know.'

That was the word which brought Donna swiftly to her senses.

Baby. It was a real word in the way that 'pregnancy' wasn't real. She couldn't put it off any longer. She had to tell him.

As soon as she got back to the tea-room she rang up the hotel before she could change her mind.

The phone was answered by a sexy female voice—all low and husky and French. Donna couldn't imagine the owner of that voice being stupid enough to find herself in the situation that *she* was in.

'Hello, this is The New Hampshire Hotel, Francine speaking. How may I 'elp you?'

'Um, I'd like to speak to Marcus Foreman.'

'And your name, please?'

'It's King. Donna King.' She had a short, humiliating wait before the voice came back.

'I am very sorry, madam, but Mr Foreman is very busy at the moment. Can I take a message?'

Donna was tempted to hang up. Or shout. Or swear. But it wasn't Francine's fault. She drew a deep breath instead. 'Could you tell him to contact me, please? I need to speak to him. Urgently.'

'That's all?'

All? How much more did she want? 'Yes, thank you. That's all.'

'He knows your number?'

'He knows where I live. The number is in the book.' And Donna hung up and went to put the hot water urn on.

He arrived that same day, when she was hanging the 'Closed' sign in the window. He was wearing a grey sweater with his black jeans, and he looked curiously sombre. Donna opened the door to him, thinking that he was going to look even more sombre in a few minutes' time.

'Hello, Marcus.' She managed a smile. 'Come in.'

'Hello, Donna,' he said warily.

He didn't say anything else until they were in her small sitting room upstairs. He looked around him, as if checking that nobody else was in the room.

'I was surprised to get your call.'

'But you didn't,' she said archly. 'Remember? You refused to take it.'

'I was in the middle of a meeting. I'm up to my eyes with plans for opening the new hotel, remember—as well as having a business to run—'

'So do I!'

He gave a short laugh. 'This is chicken-feed in comparison—and I'm not being insulting—'

'Yes, you are!'

He sighed, realising that he'd been right to stay away. 'You see? This is what happens whenever we get together, Donna. We fight—or fall into bed.'

'We never used to fight,' said Donna sadly. 'So what changed?'

Marcus shook his head as though she was being especially gullible. 'I can tell you exactly. It happened once we became involved physically—it's as simple as that. That's what changed our friendship. Sex changes everything, Donna—didn't you know that?'

Donna started feeling nervous. 'Er, yes, it certainly does.'

He looked at her. 'So?' And, on meeting her confused look, elaborated, 'Why did you want to see me?'

'Do you want to sit down? Shall I make us some tea first?' Suddenly any activity seemed preferable to having to tell him her news.

'No. Thank you.' His body had altered, it was full of

tension now, as though his senses had already alerted him of the danger to come.

What way was there to tell him? How on earth could she break it to him softly?

'I'm pregnant,' said Donna bluntly.

He was silent for no more than a split-second. 'Congratulations,' he said evenly. 'Who's the lucky man?'

Donna stared at him. 'Pardon?'

'The father,' he explained. 'Of your child.'

Donna shook her head in disbelief and the French plait felt as heavy as lead as it snaked down her spine. Even in her very worst nightmares she could never have dreamed that he would be so insensitive.

'Why, you are—of course.'

The expression in his eyes was chilling. 'There's no "of course" about it. In fact, as a candidate, I'm least likely to be the father, surely? We used a condom. Remember?'

'Candidate?' She selected the one word which had jarred more than anything else he had said and repeated it incredulously, trying to steady the rapid rise in her breathing. 'Are you...?' She struggled to complete the sentence. 'Are you implying what I think you're implying? That any number of men could be the father?'

He shrugged. 'You tell me.'

Donna resisted the desire to flail her fingernails at his mocking, sarcastic face—something she couldn't even blame on her rocketing hormones. She'd wanted to do something very similar that day when...when he had made that remark about changing the sheets after Tony Paxman had arrived.

Suddenly she got a glimmering of the way his warped mind was working, and she felt quite violently sick.

Her hand flew to her mouth and her words were muffled as a consequence. 'You don't honestly think that I jumped straight from your bed into Tony Paxman's?'

'But you weren't *in* my bed, were you, Donna? You never have been. The action all took place here. Who knows what followed next? I didn't exactly have to mount a long and strategic campaign to seduce you, did I? Why should I flatter myself that Tony Paxman would be any different?'

Donna stared at him, feeling like an animal that had been shot and wounded. Enough to traumatise but not enough to inflict a mortal blow.

Was this what had she agonised over for days and days and weeks and weeks? Was this why she had felt honour-bound to tell him? For *this*?

She felt her knees begin to give way. Saw the bright, blurry stars which danced across her line of vision like a Jackson Pollock painting. Her body was a burning core but her forehead was icy with sweat, and when she spoke her words were almost unintelligible.

'Get out! Go on—out!' she croaked, and sat down abruptly on the sofa and shut her eyes with exhaustion.

When she opened them again Marcus was bending over her, flapping a glossy magazine over her face in an attempt to circulate the air.

His own face, she noted with some satisfaction, was tight with tension.

She tried to sit up, but he shook his head and restrained her, with the flat of his hand pushed gently against one shoulder.

She wriggled like a captive eel. 'Keep your hands off me!'

'It's a little late in the day for that, surely?' was his wry reply. 'Would you like something to drink?'

'I feel like a good, stiff brandy if you must know!'

'Well, you can't have it,' he answered repressively. 'Not in your condition.'

'Condition?' Donna nearly burst into noisy sobs. 'It's such a corny word!'

'It's a pretty corny situation all round,' he said bitterly, and turned towards the door.

'Where are you going?' she choked.

'To make you some tea. *I'll* have the brandy.'

She stretched out on the sofa until the shuddering of her breathing became steady, and she must have drifted off into a light sleep, because when she opened her eyes it was to find Marcus pouring out tea and spooning sugar into it.

'I told you I'd given up sugar,' she said tiredly.

'Shut up,' he answered, but his voice was almost gentle.

She still felt lousy. Physically. And yet some of the burden seemed to have been lifted from her shoulders. He hadn't actually told her not to worry, and she didn't think he would—but at least she didn't feel alone any more.

He waited until she had drunk some tea and a little colour had returned to her face. Then he sat down on a hard chair opposite her.

'So. You say I'm the father?'

She shook her head. 'No. I don't *say*, Marcus—you *are* the father.'

'Are you sure?'

She finished her tea and put the cup down on the carpet. It was no good feeling offended by his assumptions—she hadn't exactly behaved like some sort of saint, had she? But one thing was for sure—if she started behaving hysterically it would not do anyone any good.

Least of all the baby.

She placed a protective palm over her belly, and if Marcus registered the sudden action he didn't comment on it. 'Quite sure,' she said calmly.

He cleared his throat. 'May I ask how?'

'Didn't you do biology at school?' she questioned wildly.

'Don't be flippant at a time like this! I asked you a civil question—I'd appreciate a civil answer!'

'Because…' She floundered for the most delicate way of phrasing it—but what was the point? They'd insulted each other about as much as they could. 'Because you're the only man I've had sex with.' She saw that he still looked unconvinced.

'Since when?'

'A long time,' she said emphatically. 'A very long time.' He still didn't look convinced. 'For…oh, for at least a couple of years.'

He nodded. 'Oh, I see. One of the condoms must have split,' he said to himself. 'How many times did we do it?'

Donna blushed. 'I don't remember.'

'That's probably how it happened,' he sighed. 'Don't they say that human—?'

'Stop it!' She clapped her hands over her ears as she glared at him in outrage. 'I do not need to hear how wonderfully adaptable the human sperm is at a time like this!'

'No,' he agreed slowly, and looked up, the ice-blue eyes looking troubled. 'How far gone are you?'

The words didn't seem to make any sense. She stared at him blankly.

'How many weeks are you?'

'Nearly twenty-two.'

There was a long, loaded silence. His eyes met hers

incredulously. 'You're that advanced?' he asked in a shocked voice.

'Think about it, Marcus. You could have worked it out for yourself!' she retorted.

'You mean it's been that long, since...since we...?'

'Made love?' she questioned. He probably wouldn't have described it that way himself—but now that there was a tiny life growing inside her she needed to feel that the act of creating that life had been more than just sex. 'Yes. It is.'

He was shaking his head as if he had just come out of some long-term trance. Surely it couldn't have been that long ago? Had over twenty-two weeks really passed since he'd told himself that no matter how tempted he was—he wasn't going to go near her again?

'Listen,' he grated. 'Maths is usually my strong point—but not right at this moment. My head is spinning.' The ice-blue eyes burned with a strange kind of intensity. 'Just tell me when the baby is due.'

'Early in the New Year. The first week of January,' she told him at last, and as the words came tumbling out she thought that she had never seen him look quite so shattered by anything.

'You're kidding?'

'I wish I was.'

The blue eyes bored into her. 'And what's that supposed to mean?'

Donna looked at him. What did he expect her to say? That she was overjoyed at the thought of bringing an unplanned child into the world? A child whose father thought so little of her that he had not been near her since that afternoon of passion more than five months ago? 'I don't know what I mean,' she said. 'I'm mixed up, I guess.'

Marcus found his eyes drawn irresistibly to her stomach. He realised that he had only ever looked at a woman's body as an object of desire before now, but suddenly he recognised that Donna's body would nurture his child. He swallowed, the enormity of it all hitting him as he looked closer, but he could detect no tell-tale swell. Not underneath that loose shirt she was wearing.

'God, I could do with a drink.'

'Then have one.'

'No, I'd better not.' He looked at his watch and sighed. 'I have to go out tonight. Very soon, in fact.'

'And that's the difference between us, isn't it?' she questioned, and her voice was filled with a kind of bitterness as she felt her freedom begin to slip away. 'Your life will go on undisturbed, won't it, Marcus?'

'Well, hardly,' he bit out. 'I can't imagine that I'm going to have a rip-roaring time tonight after this bombshell has been dropped in my lap.'

'You're concerned about your social *calendar*?' she demanded incredulously. 'Don't worry about me—I'm just concerned about the rest of my life!'

'For God's sake, will you stop twisting my words, Donna? I was thinking short-term, that's all. You were looking at the wider canvas. Understandably.'

She knew that she had no right to ask where he was going, or with whom, and yet stupidly enough she felt as though she *did* have rights. He was the father of her unborn child, for heaven's sake!

But only through luck. Or bad luck, as he would probably see it. Luck he could have done without.

Donna made her mind up in that moment. This baby had not been conceived out of love. Certainly not on Marcus's part. But one thing was for sure—when their child arrived kicking and shouting into the world in the New Year there would be nothing but love waiting.

She sat up, feeling stronger now, smoothing back a damp tendril of hair. She leaned back against the cushions. 'Maybe it's best if we get a few things straight right from the start, Marcus.'

He became watchful. 'Go on,' he said warily.

'I just want you to know that I'm not asking you for financial support.'

He stilled. 'Oh?'

'And I'm not asking for your emotional support, either.'

'Really?' His eyes burned into her. 'Just what *are* you asking, then, Donna?'

'Nothing.' She bit her lip. 'Nothing at all.'

'No money? No babysitting for the nights you want to go out?'

She couldn't project that far into the future; she simply couldn't imagine it. 'That's right.'

'So why bother telling me at all?'

Surely he understood that? 'Because as the father you have a right to know.'

'Just no right to have any involvement with my son or daughter's life?'

'But you wouldn't want any, surely?' she asked him, her surprise genuine.

'How the hell do you know what I want—when I don't even know myself?' he snarled. 'And how can I possibly make a snap decision about such an earth-shattering piece of information as this?'

'Marcus—'

'I want time to think about it,' he continued remorselessly. 'We've already acted with indecent haste—maybe if we hadn't then we wouldn't have found ourselves in this situation. We owe it to the baby to work out our best options. *And we owe it to ourselves,*' he finished quietly.

Even in the midst of all the emotions which swirled around her like the thrashing sea above the head of a non-swimmer, two words pushed themselves to the front of her mind.

The baby. How cold that sounded.

'It isn't *the* baby—it's *my* baby,' she said aloud, in case the child growing inside her could hear them, and might turn distractedly in the womb, feeling unloved and unwanted.

'My baby, too,' he said quietly. He looked at her fierce little face and felt a pang of something approaching remorse. If only he hadn't ravished her quite so thoroughly. He swallowed down his self-disgust.

At least they were agreed on something—his behaviour *had* seemed to be way beyond control. Indeed, he could not remember ever having been so overcome with desire—but he could hardly blame her for *that*, could he? And, meanwhile, he should have been somewhere else ten minutes ago. 'Listen, this is too much to take on board and try and sort out in one brief meeting. Besides, I have to go now.'

'Of course you do.'

He stared at her. She looked so damned vulnerable, lying there. 'Will you be…all right?'

Donna forced herself to get up off the sofa, impatiently shaking off the hand which he immediately reached out to steady her. 'Of course I'll be all right. And there's no need to treat me like a fragile old lady! I'm pregnant, Marcus—not ill!'

'Yeah,' he agreed. The static in the air had made the loose shirt cling to her, and now he could see the definite curve of her belly. He felt a lump rise in his throat, and instinctively reached out and put his arms around her in a gesture of comfort.

For a moment Donna let herself be held, sinking into the warm security of his arms where she felt safe. He smelt clean—of lemons and musk—and she found that she wanted to sink into the protection of his body, to rest her head on his shoulder. In that moment she felt really close to him.

How peculiar that a simple hug could be infinitely more intimate than full-scale sex. She pulled away— knowing that it was dangerous to attach more than she should to small acts of support.

'You'd...better go.'

'Yes.' But he seemed strangely reluctant to move. 'Goodnight, Donna,' he said at last.

'When will I see you?' Funny, too, that her new-found 'condition' gave her the right to ask questions like this.

'I don't know,' he told her. 'I honestly don't know.'

CHAPTER SEVEN

JUST as soon as Marcus had left, Donna was asking herself why on earth she'd been so passive. She shouldn't have asked when she was going to see him. She should have demanded to know!

Because things needed to be decided.

Like what official story they were going to give. Winchester might be a city but it was a tiny city—known fondly by its inhabitants as the village with a cathedral! And as the pregnancy became more advanced they were going to have to say *something*. She wouldn't be able to keep it secret from Ally or Sarah for much longer either, that was for sure.

Oddly enough, the subject came up the following morning. Donna had been baking scones in the kitchen since six. Just lately the sickness seemed to come late-morning, and she found that if she could get the bulk of the food preparation over before that then she was usually free of the horrible, dry retching which made her stomach feel like a deflated balloon afterwards.

But this morning the sickness had struck early, and without warning. Donna wondered if it was the psychological impact of having told Marcus and consequently not sleeping a wink all night. By the time Ally came in just after nine—when she'd dropped her daughter Charlotte off at school—Donna was sitting white-faced and trembling at the kitchen table.

Ally took one look at her pinched face and grimaced. 'Tea?'

'Yuck! No!' moaned Donna.

'Sympathy, then?'

'Sympathy is just a word.' Donna shrugged listlessly. 'It doesn't actually do or change anything.'

'No, it doesn't,' agreed Ally calmly. 'But it might just make you feel better.'

Donna shook her head. 'I can't.'

'Can't what? Can't face up to fact that you're going to have a baby?'

Donna stared across the table at her in dry-eyed shock. 'How on earth did you know?' she whispered.

'How?' Ally gave a short laugh. 'I'm a mother myself! I've suspected for weeks, if you must know. It's harder than you think to hide pregnancy, you know, Donna—particularly from another woman.'

'Oh, God,' groaned Donna, and leaned onto the table, resting her head wearily on her arms. 'What am I going to do?'

'You don't really have a lot of choices, do you?' asked Ally crisply. 'How many weeks are you? About twenty?'

'Bit more,' mumbled Donna against her forearms.

'Well, in that case you're obviously going to have to go ahead and have the baby—'

Donna sat up, her expression one of outrage. 'Of course I'm going to go ahead and have the baby!' she stormed. 'Why ever would you think—?'

'Shh!' soothed Ally. 'Keep your hair on! I didn't mean to offend you, or to suggest anything—it's just that a lot of women in your situation would have considered—'

'Don't even say it!' warned Donna, and then her eyes narrowed suspiciously. 'What situation?'

Ally shrugged. 'You're not with the father, I take it?'

'Is it that obvious?'

'Yes.'

'Oh, Ally, I feel so *stupid*! How did I ever get myself into this position?'

'Donna,' Ally sighed. 'You're no more stupid than countless other women have been. These things happen. Have you told him? The father, I mean.'

'Yes.' Donna stared at the table. 'I've told him.'

'And what does he say?'

'That we have to talk about it.'

'That's very good of him,' said Ally drily, and then she creased her nose up. 'I don't suppose there's any chance of the two of you ever—?'

'No,' said Donna firmly. 'None whatsoever. He's made that perfectly clear.' She picked a rosy apple out of the fruit bowl and began to rub it absently against her sleeve, but then another wave of nausea hit her and she quickly put it back. 'You haven't asked me whether he's married.'

'Why should I ask that?'

'Well, it is an obvious assumption to make when a woman has a lover that no one has ever seen. Isn't it?'

'But I know he's not married,' said Ally slowly. 'Marcus Foreman is the father, isn't he?' She saw Donna's dazed expression and gave a short laugh. 'And before you ask, no—I'm not a mind-reader. It was just pretty obvious to me—and to Sarah.'

Donna silently filed away the fact that the two of them must have discussed it. 'How? When I haven't seen him for weeks?'

'You were so distracted after he came to see you the day we opened. You used to jump six feet in the air and snatch the phone up whenever it rang. Then your face would crumple when you discovered it was the wholesalers asking about a jam delivery! But not for long. There was always that gritty smile lying in wait.' Her face softened. 'You were always determined not to look upset when the bastard didn't ring you.'

'He is not a bastard,' defended Donna dully.

'Maybe his mother and father were legally married,' conceded Ally. 'But he's behaved like one towards you, hasn't he?'

'Actually, no.'

'Donna—now you're just being soft!'

But Donna shook her head. 'I'm not. If he really *was* an out-and-out bastard he would have visited me on more than one occasion, instead of just the once. Some men would have done that if there was sex without questions on offer. At least this way he wasn't pretending to feel something he obviously didn't. He made me feel like a mistake, not a prostitute.'

The two of them stiffened as they heard the sound of a key in the lock.

Donna looked at Ally. 'So Sarah knows, too?'

'Yes. She guessed herself. You've been wearing shapeless tops for ages now. And, like I say, it's pretty obvious to another woman.'

'I would have told you weeks ago, except that I was too scared to acknowledge it, even to myself. And I felt I couldn't tell anyone—not until I'd told Marcus.' Donna heard the sound of the telephone ringing, and Sarah's voice calling to say that she would answer it. 'Listen, Ally—please don't say a word to anyone else. Not until I've discussed it again with Marcus.'

'Don't worry, I won't.'

They both looked up as Sarah came to the door, an expectant smile on her face.

'Mmm,' she said pointedly. 'Guess who's on the phone for *you*, Donna?'

'The taxman?'

'Marcus Foreman.'

Donna tried not to look as though she was rushing, but she was puffing slightly as she picked up the receiver. 'Hello?'

'Why are you out of breath?' demanded the voice at the other end.

'Because pregnant women get easily puffed!'

There was a pause while he considered this. 'Will you have dinner with me tonight?'

'Dinner?'

He gave a short laugh. 'Is that such a bizarre request in the circumstances, Donna?'

She heard the sarcasm which coloured his voice and understood it immediately. If there had been a time for sounding shocked it should have been when he had arrived wearing a dark, sultry expression and intent on seduction. Not when he was asking her to share a meal with him as two civilised and consenting adults.

'No, of course it isn't,' she told him quickly. She was about to utter, I'd love to, but that would have been pure convention, not truth. 'Where?'

Another pause. 'I thought at my house.'

She bit her lip. 'The New Hampshire too public for you?'

'Not in the way you're thinking—'

'And how the hell would you know what I was thinking, Marcus?'

He sighed. 'If we go to a restaurant—and that's any restaurant, not just mine—then we're on show, aren't we? People watch us, assess us.'

'Assess *me*, you mean. And how pregnant I am.'

'Donna,' he said patiently. 'Unless you've suddenly been diagnosed as expecting triplets I can't for the life of me see how yesterday your pregnancy was a secret whilst today the whole world would know that secret just by looking at you!'

'Because today I really *feel* pregnant!' she wailed.

'Probably because you told someone,' he mused. 'Anyway, dinner. Come early—is six o'clock okay?'

'I suppose so.'

'Do you want me to come and collect you?'

'No, I think I can probably manage the five-minute walk myself.'

'Well, if you're sure...'

'Marcus, I'm not an *invalid*—I told you that before!'

'No,' he agreed. 'You're just having a baby. My baby, in fact,' he finished, with an unfamiliar note of something she couldn't quite put her finger on. And Donna wondered whether it had been pride or panic she had heard in his voice.

Donna had dressed carefully the day she had got her licence and taken Tony Paxman out for lunch—but that had been nothing compared to the agonised deliberations she indulged in once she'd shut up shop and sent Sarah and Ally home. Dinner with Marcus in the most bizarre circumstances imaginable—so what did she wear?

The sleek cream dress and matching jacket she had worn that day were immediately rejected as much too formal. Donna narrowed her eyes at the dress and guessed that it probably wouldn't do up any more, anyway.

Given her newly expanded waistline, she didn't really have a lot of choice. Pencil skirts were out, for obvious reasons. So were the narrowly cut trousers she sometimes wore. And what self-destructive little imp had prompted her to think that she might be able to get away with jeans and a big cotton T-shirt?

She couldn't even get the jeans past her thighs! This was worse than the days when she was a teenager and used to have to lie on the floor and use a coat-hanger to lever the skin-tight denim flaps together! She was definitely going to have to buy some new clothes to accommodate this baby.

In the end she selected a simple silk trouser suit which she had bought and worn to death when she had lived in New Zealand. The wide, soft trousers had an elasticated waistband and the slip-over top was cool and roomy. She'd washed it more times than she cared to remember, and it had faded from deepest cinnamon to pale topaz. But it still looked good. It hid the swell of her belly and the colour made the most of her pale skin and orange-red hair and green eyes.

She put on a coat of waterproof mascara and a slick of clear lipgloss, then wove a black velvet ribbon into the French plait and she was ready.

Marcus lived in a road just behind the hotel, where the houses were detached and elegant, their gardens shimmering pockets of well-tended lawns with carefully chosen shrubs spilling onto their gravelled paths. It was a balmy evening, the air thick with the scent of roses and the muted sound of a late tennis game somewhere in the distance.

Marcus opened the door before she had a chance to ring the bell, which she guessed meant that he had been watching out for her—and that pleased her. Not because she thought for a moment that he was mooning over her like a lovesick calf—but because it implied that he was nervous, too. Which would even things up a little. And it wasn't like Marcus to be nervous.

He stood in the doorway and looked at her. Despite what he'd said to her on the phone about looking no different he realised that she *did* look different. How you saw someone depended on what you thought about them. And now he knew she was pregnant she suddenly looked like the most pregnant woman in the world. Cool and clean as a glass of water. All glowing and growing and radiant.

'Hi,' he said, and his voice sounded much softer than usual. 'Glad you could make it. Come in.'

'Thanks.' Glad she could *make* it? Heavens, how *formal* they sounded—as though it was a boardroom meeting they were attending. And how surreal—given the circumstances of why she was there!

She stepped into the wide hallway, with its sweeping staircase and softly gleaming wooden banister, and felt herself suddenly cloaked with insecurities.

Marcus noticed her body freeze with tension, and he frowned. 'Is something the matter?'

She shrugged. 'It's a little strange being here, that's all. I mean, I've never even set foot over the threshold of your house before, not in all the time I worked for you. I was never invited, and I suppose I never would have been invited either, if I hadn't got myself into this awkward situation.'

His face darkened. 'I think we have to take joint responsibility for the "awkward situation", as you so sweetly put it. As for never coming here.' He gave her a look which was the closest she had ever seen to Marcus looking helpless. 'There was never any reason for you to come here, was there? That wasn't the way things were. How they worked.'

'No, I guess not. You were the boss and I was the chambermaid.' She'd only ever seen him at the hotel. The world had not seemed to exist outside the hotel. It had become their world in microcosm.

Marcus had been working all the hours that God sent. And he'd needed to. His father had been sick and frail for a long time before his death, but he'd been a stubborn man. He hadn't been able to bear to relinquish his control of the family business to his son, even though he hadn't really been fit to run it himself.

And it had only been after his death that Marcus had discovered the disastrous state of the hotel's finances and had set about trying to salvage them.

'And was I a good boss?' he asked suddenly.

He had been a very distracting boss.

'You never seemed to go home,' she said, remembering the time when she had started work one morning and found him fast asleep at his office desk. She'd crept away and made a tray of coffee and put it on his desk before gently shaking his shoulder. He'd woken sleepily, and rubbed his eyes, and an odd, jolting kind of stare had passed between them while a blistering silence had ticked away around them, like a time-bomb.

And that was the precise moment that Donna had decided she was falling in love with him...

'You were the original workaholic.' She smiled wistfully at the memory.

He studied the careful way that she answered him, sensing that he couldn't hold back on this—it just wasn't fair to her. 'I never wanted to go home,' he said simply. 'You made working late the most attractive prospect I could imagine...well, nearly,' he added, then wished he hadn't. If there was one thing he *wasn't* going to do tonight it was to treat her like a sex object.

'Come through,' he said—and gestured towards a door at the end of the corridor. 'To the kitchen.'

It was a huge kitchen, with a big, scrubbed pine table and an enormous old-fashioned range. It looked too tidy to be a room which was used a lot, and Donna wondered how often he ate here. But there were some beautiful pieces of coloured glass dotted here and there, and a terracotta dish containing oranges and lemons. She could imagine a cat sitting contentedly by the range. A ginger cat, licking its glossy coat.

'It's a beautiful room,' she murmured.

The French windows were open, leading out onto a garden which was still a blur of mauves and pinks and blues, although the brilliant greens of high summer were gone. Donna blinked. Were those really children's voices she could hear—or had she imagined those as well?

She turned round to find Marcus studying her intently.

'What would you like to drink?' he asked. 'I've got most fruit juices. Or there's mineral water, if you'd prefer.'

The feeling of losing control over her body was only intensified. Donna frowned at him. 'And what would you say if I asked you for a proper drink? A glass of wine or a beer?'

'I'd probably tell you that although one or two drinks a week are permissible after the first trimester, doctors now recommend—'

'Marcus!' Donna dropped her handbag onto a high-backed chair which stood next to the range and turned indignantly to face him. 'Will you stop it?'

'Stop what?'

'Trying to take control!'

'I wasn't,' he said stubbornly. 'I was just—'

'Yes, I know! Interfering! It's my body,' she declared.

'And you've got my baby growing inside it,' he told her quietly.

Wide-eyed, they stared at one another, his words shocking them both into silence.

Marcus had spent a sleepless night trying to come to terms with her news. Yesterday he had been dazed and confused. And angry. But this morning he'd found himself standing in his garden to see the new dawn break—his feet all bare and soaked with dew. And what had seemed like an out-and-out disaster in the darkest hours had taken on an air of mystery and wonder as the sun had burst upon the sky in a blaze of pink and orange and purple.

A baby...

But that had still been a baby in the abstract sense. Saying those words out loud somehow made it real. And far more real for her than for him. She was the one it was actually happening to. What right did he have to police her every move?

'Have a glass of wine if you'd like some,' he growled.

'I wouldn't, actually,' she answered sweetly. 'But I'd like to be given the choice. You see, over the years I've become rather fond of making my own decisions!'

'Point taken, Donna.' He gave a slightly unsteady smile as he poured out two tall glasses of mineral water, adding ice and lemon before handing her one. 'So. What shall we drink to?' he asked. 'The baby?'

'The baby.' She nodded obediently, wondering if this sensation of unreality would ever disappear. It was as if this was all happening to someone else, not her. She stole a glance at the calm way he was sipping at his drink. 'You seem to have accepted the fact remarkably well.'

'I don't have a choice, do I?' He put his drink down and slid some bread into the oven, then bent to take salad ingredients from out of the fridge and began chopping tomatoes. 'And when you don't have a choice—then you make the best of things. Good lesson for life.'

She thought that, yes, it was. That in a funny kind of way that had been exactly her own philosophy—right from when she had been a little girl. She looked up to tell him that and found his eyes on her, the flash of understanding in them telling her far more clearly than words ever could that he knew.

He put the knife down, and smiled as he said her name, the smile all mixed up with tenderness and regret. 'Oh, Donna,' he sighed.

His eyes were incandescent with a fierce blue light, and for a moment she nearly forgot herself. Nearly reached across and touched her fingertips against the faint shadow on his chin. Wanting to trace the shape of his face, the squared-off curve of his jaw, the sensual pout of his lips. But she had no right to touch him, none at all, and she shrank back.

'What is it?' he demanded urgently. 'Why has your face gone so white? Is it the baby? Are you sick?'

She shook her head. 'No. I just got a short, sharp dose of reality which forced me to accept a few unpalatable facts.'

He severed a piece of cucumber. 'Oh?'

'I remembered that I am only here by accident. That's all. We are not partners, Marcus, not in the true sense of the word. Nor even lovers. And I am not the proud bearer of your child—I am simply a vessel that got filled by—'

'Don't you dare!' He put the knife down and gripped

her upper arms—not hard, but she could feel his fingers burning into her flesh through the thin silk.

'Don't dare tell the truth, you mean?'

He shook his head impatiently. 'That's only your version of the truth. Thinking negatively won't do you any good at all,' he ground out. 'Or the baby. Or the whole damn situation!'

He moved his face closer, and Donna felt helpless beneath a gaze so probing it made her feel that he could look into her mind and read every thought there.

Could he tell that she wanted him with an urgency which had her fingers itching to pull his face down to hers? To meet and meld with those sweet, hard lips which would open under pressure... She swallowed down her desire with difficulty and wriggled out of his grip.

'We have to be positive,' he whispered. 'Both of us.'

She nodded her head. 'I know we do.'

His eyes blazed. 'I don't want you to worry, Donna. Not about anything. Do you understand?'

The attack of lust passed as quickly as it had arrived, in time for her to realise that he was talking to her as if she had just had her brain removed.

'But I'm not worried!' she protested. 'Honestly!'

He shook his head, as if he thought she was just reassuring him for the sake of it, to be polite. 'Well, I am,' he said flatly.

'You're worried?'

'Yes, I am.'

She looked at him expectantly. 'What about?'

'About you living in that flat above the tea-room, for a start.'

Donna fixed him with a furious look. He hadn't

thought the flat so ghastly that it had prevented him making love to her there! 'What's wrong with it?'

'Well, imagine if your kitchen caught fire!' he said heatedly.

Donna frowned. 'Why should it?'

'Because you're living above the kitchen! You cook food in larger than average quantities, don't you? You employ staff, don't you? Therefore the possibilities of some kind of fire breaking out are much greater. Good grief, your oven could explode!'

'And so could yours!' she retorted. 'I've had the premises checked by the environmental and safety officers! I'm not living in a booby-trap, you know!'

'I'm not suggesting you are—'

'And for your information, I check the kitchens myself, every single night before I go around locking up.'

'Exactly!' He beamed with triumph. 'It's too much for you to handle! You're doing that now and you look exhausted, if you want the truth. Imagine when you're dragging yourself around at forty weeks.'

'You're making me sound like an Atlantic whale!' Donna objected mildly. But she was surprised and impressed that he knew how long a pregnancy lasted, and remembered his earlier pat comments about 'the first trimester'. 'And since when did you become such an expert on childbirth?'

He gave an unfamiliar and sheepish grin. 'I went out and bought just about every book there was on the subject.'

'And how many was that?' she asked faintly.

He counted off on his fingers. 'Four books on pregnancy. There's an even bigger section on the first year of life, and then—'

'I've heard everything I need to know.'

'Ah, but that's where you're wrong!' He poured them out some more mineral water, as if playing for time. 'Whatever objections you may put up, you know in your heart that I'm right.'

'If you say so, Marcus,' she said demurely, thinking that if she gave him enough rope he might hang himself!

He breezed on, not seeming to notice her sceptical expression. 'And The Buttress—whilst being an excellent tea-room—' he crinkled an encouraging smile at her '—and I'm impressed with what you've done, believe me.'

'Gee, thanks!'

If he heard the sardonic note in her voice, he didn't react to it. 'But it is *not* the place for a pregnant woman, and neither is it the place for a brand-new baby. And that's why I've decided—' he drew a deep breath, like a man seeking courage to make the ultimate sacrifice '—to let you come and live here.'

CHAPTER EIGHT

DONNA was so thunderstruck by Marcus's suggestion that she just stared at him, her mouth limply falling open. She must have misheard. *Must* have.

'I'm not sure I heard that properly, Marcus.'

He smiled the complacent smile of a man who had never been turned down for anything in his life. 'You can come and live here,' he explained kindly. 'My home will become your home.'

'When you say *live* here...' Donna hesitated as quiet hysteria gave her the terrible temptation to giggle. She tried to find a diplomatic way of wording her question and realised that there wasn't one. 'What do you mean, exactly?'

His eyes were wary. 'It sounds straightforward enough to me.'

'Well, not to me. I'm interested to know just what role I'd be expected to play.'

'What role?' he repeated cautiously.

'Sure. Will I be your partner, in the full sense of the word? Will we be sharing a bed and having sex together? Or am I simply expected to drift around the edges of your life? And, in that case, won't your girlfriends be rather spooked when they see a woman who is heavily pregnant—with your child—walking around the place and treating it like home. What if I unwittingly walked in just as you were about to seduce one of them on the sofa?'

'Donna!'

113

'It's no good saying "Donna!" like that,' she said serenely, enjoying the look of outrage on his face. 'That doesn't answer any of my questions.'

'Do you really think that I'd be upstairs…?' His voice trailed off in disbelief and it took a moment or two for him to repeat the word. 'Upstairs…'

'Making love?' she put in helpfully, feeling emotionally stronger by the second. 'Well, that would certainly be preferable to you being *downstairs* making love!'

'Just what kind of a man do you think I am?' he demanded.

'Well, since you ask…' Donna met his gaze unflinchingly. 'The kind of man who has sex when he feels like it and doesn't even bother seeing the woman afterwards. Does that sound familiar?'

'Oh. Oh, I see.' His watchfulness transformed itself into a panther-like stealth, and Donna wondered if she had pushed him just a little too far.

'Is that what this is all about?' he queried silkily. 'The fact that it was just a one-off? Is that why you're so angry?'

'I thought I was being more practical than angry,' she reasoned, because anger would imply vulnerability—and she needed to be strong. 'I've learnt to cope with most things in my life, Marcus, and this won't be any different.' She shrugged her shoulders. 'These things happen.'

'Especially to us. One-night stands seem to be our speciality, don't they, sugar?'

He reached his hand up towards her face and Donna tensed, but he was merely brushing a strand of hair from where it had been threatening to glue itself to her lips.

The tiny gesture was oddly touching. It made her feel defenceless when she needed to be tough. Did he recognise that? Was that why he had renewed his campaign?

'And you still haven't answered my question.' He studied her carefully. 'About coming to live here.'

Donna moved away from the work-top, wanting to be out of range of that delectable ice-blue stare, but wanting more than anything to eat. These days she seemed to be controlled by her body.

She smiled at him. 'I can't possibly answer that on an empty stomach. So, can we please have some food now? I'm starving.'

Marcus gave a small, wry smile in response. Had he thought she would agree to come and live here as easily as she had agreed to have such warm and beautiful sex with him? 'Sure we can.' He added some tuna to the salad and took the warmed bread out of the oven. 'Want to eat in here? Or is it warm enough to eat outside?'

'Outside.'

'Then let's go.'

Donna carried out the checkered cloth he gave her and spread it over the grass, while Marcus carried the food and water on a tray.

He spooned her out a generous portion of salade niçoise and watched while she devoured it with an appetite which took him right back to that day when she had arrived—so cold and wet and hungry. And the sense of protectiveness he'd felt towards her then was nothing to what he was experiencing right now.

'Do you always eat that much these days?' he enquired, once she had paused for breath.

She wiped up the last of the dressing with a piece of bread and ate it slowly, waiting until she had finished chewing before she answered his question. 'Not usually. It's this pregnancy business.'

He turned onto his side and stretched out on the grass, tucking the white T-shirt into his jeans as he did so, making Donna horribly aware of how long and how muscular his legs were.

'So, tell me all about it,' he said softly. 'This pregnancy business.'

She pushed her empty plate away and took a sip of water. 'Sometimes you're so sick that you tell yourself you'll never eat another thing—just so you won't be able to be sick.'

'And then?'

She shrugged. 'Then the baby must send some message to your brain, or your stomach—or something. Because suddenly you discover that you could devour just about everything in the fridge—and then some! You feel like one of those locusts you see on nature films— the kind that march around stripping everything bare...' Now why had she said *that*?

His eyes darkened at the way she faltered on those last few words, and his smile grew thoughtful. 'Well, feel free, Donna,' he murmured. 'Strip everything bare, if that's what you really want.'

She glared. 'It isn't really helpful if you're going to make suggestive remarks like that, Marcus.'

'It's the effect you're having on me,' he groaned.

'But I'm not doing anything!' she protested.

'No?' He suspected that if she started reading from the telephone directory he would find it sexy! 'Don't look so shocked! Surely you must realise how damned gorgeous you look sitting there?'

'*Gorgeous?*' She looked down at herself. All she could see was the swollen breasts and tummy, which, after the gigantic portion of food she had just put away, made it look as though she was due to give birth at any moment.

'Normally I can't stand false modesty—but that

sounds pretty genuine to me.' He shook his head in disbelief. 'Of course you look gorgeous. You're blooming, Donna,' he said softly. 'Blooming like a rose in high summer. Your skin is clear and your eyes are bright as stars. Hell, your figure has always been the best I've ever seen on any woman, but pregnancy has only enhanced it.'

He shut up then. Her mutinous expression told him that now might not be a good time to tell her how magnificent her breasts looked. He rolled over onto his stomach. At least that way there was a chance she wouldn't notice just how she was affecting him. Or where.

Donna saw him wince and thought she knew why. She'd seen the flush which had heightened his colour, emphasising those amazing cheekbones. The hectic glitter in his eyes hadn't gone unnoticed, either. She found herself wanting to touch him. To run her fingertips over the satin of his skin, seeking out all the dark and secret hollows.

She thought how easy it would be to lie back beside him. To pretend that she needed to digest her meal. Or to look at the clouds as they chased one another across the sky. Then it would be only a matter of time before he leaned over to press his mouth against hers.

And she wanted that. Wanted him. He was the only man she had *ever* wanted, in truth.

'So, are you going to come and move in with me, Donna?'

His voice sounded as disconnected as the distant droning of a lawnmower in one of the neighbouring gardens.

The eighteen-year-old Donna would have leapt at the chance, but she was no longer eighteen. Nine years on she had got herself into a crazy situation—but she didn't have to make it even crazier.

She shook her head. 'No, I'm not. I can't think of a worse idea, to be honest. I'm still trying to get used to the fact that in under four months' time I'm going to have a tiny baby to look after. Now is certainly not the right time to start experimenting by living with someone.'

He turned onto his back again, the urgency to possess her disappearing with the moment. 'I might not ask you again.'

Donna laughed. 'Oh, dear!' she teased. 'Then I've missed my chance for ever. Well, there you go!'

Marcus looked up at the darkening sky which domed above them. He couldn't figure her out. He had thought... He frowned.

Donna looked down at him. 'What's the matter, Marcus?' she taunted softly. 'Can't believe a woman has said no to you?'

He was gentle with her because she was pregnant, but there was no hesitation in his movement as he pulled her down on top of him, feeling the lush resistance of her ripening flesh against the sudden hard throbbing of his. 'Maybe I think I can change your mind,' came his soft groan as he tangled his fingers in her French plait and brought her mouth down to his.

He kissed her, and that was all he did. He didn't grapple with her clothing or try to explore the contours of her body. Just lay there with his fingers nonchalantly threaded into her hair, his lips alternatively sweet and soft and hard and hungry.

It was both passive and seeking. Innocent and immensely experienced. It was a slow, drugging seduction and it was entirely new to her.

And Donna was completely unprepared for its impact. With Marcus everything had always been so hot and immediate. As if the world would end if they didn't join their bodies together as quickly as possible. No one had ever told her it could be like *this*.

She lay dazed and unfurling on top of him, feeling the honeyed pulsing of desire as it stealthily invaded her body.

Marcus knew that he had to stop. This was unlike anything in his experience. More beautiful than anything he'd ever felt. And in a minute he'd....

Donna blinked as he tore his mouth away to somehow gather her up into his arms and gracefully manoeuvre them both to a standing position, and only when she felt the ground beneath her feet did he let her go.

'Donna—'

'You're out of breath,' she gasped.

'So are you.' He paused, still disorientated by that kiss. 'And your hair is all over the place.'

She brushed a damp curl off her cheek, feeling the sweat as it pricked her forehead. She brushed a few strands of dry grass from her sleeve and began to walk towards the house.

He walked by her side across the springy turf. 'Can I come to the clinic with you? And see the scan? I want to see the baby's heart beating.'

Suddenly she felt guilty. 'I've already had a scan.'

He tensed, knowing that he had no right to feel excluded. 'And?'

'And it all looks fine. Absolutely fine.' A smile broke out on her lips and suddenly he was smiling too, and if this had been a normal relationship she would have flung her arms around him and he would have picked her up and twirled her round like a carousel.

But it wasn't a normal relationship. And Donna realised that they had avoided discussing some very practical issues.

'People are going to start noticing soon,' she said.

'Hasn't anyone noticed already?'

'Ally has. And Sarah. But neither of them has said anything. What do you want me to say, if anyone asks?'

Marcus studied her. She was asking his opinion and yet he didn't count, not really. She'd made love to him and was carrying his child as a consequence. Then she had lain kissing on the grass with him—but now he offered to do the decent thing and *live* with her she didn't want to know.

'Marcus?' She butted into his thoughts. 'What do you want me to tell people?'

He felt the anger rising up inside him, and he turned his face away, so that all she could see was a shadowed profile etched softly against the dusky evening light. 'That's entirely up to you.'

She wished he would help her out. Did he enjoy seeing her have to ask these humiliating questions? 'So if I tell people that you're the...father—you won't mind?'

'Why should I? They're going to find out soon enough,' he said flatly. 'Because as soon as the baby is born I shall be applying for custody.'

CHAPTER NINE

'HE SAID *what*?'

Donna willed herself to stop shaking for long enough to repeat what she had just told an incredulous Ally.

'Marcus said...' She took a great gulping breath of air which steadied her voice. 'That he was going to fight me for custody of the baby once he or she is born.'

'But he can't do that,' said Ally.

'Who says he can't? He can do any damn thing he pleases. He's rich. He's powerful. He's influential. What judge isn't going to look at him and compare him favourably to me—a girl from the wrong side of the tracks. Struggling to start her own business and to bring a baby up at the same time.' Donna groaned. 'What about the current backlash against working mothers? The belief that women who put their careers before their babies are uncaring?'

'But you aren't *planning* to put the tea-room before the baby, are you?' questioned Ally patiently.

Donna carried on as if she hadn't heard her. 'There's a big swing in favour of fathers at the moment—you know there is. Fathers are clamouring to be heard—saying that they are just as capable of bringing up a child as the mother. Oh, Ally,' she wailed. 'What am I going to do?'

Ally glowered. 'You can stop acting like you've already lost—that's for sure! Then you take yourself off to a lawyer and you find out exactly where you stand!

121

You know a lawyer, don't you? The guy who brought the champagne round the day we opened?'

'Tony Paxman,' said Donna dully.

'Well, then. He's a friend, isn't he?'

'Not really.'

Donna didn't feel like explaining to Ally that Tony Paxman hadn't really been offering the only kind of friendship she would accept. And somehow she didn't imagine he would look very favourably on the fact that she was expecting Marcus's baby. 'Oh, I just don't know what to do,' she sighed. 'I really don't.'

'Well, I *do*!' said Ally firmly. 'You have all the power in this, Donna—just think about it. You're pregnant, aren't you? *You're* the one carrying the baby. And you're looking after yourself—anyone can see that. Okay,' she amended, as she noticed the huge, dark shadows beneath Donna's eyes, 'you don't look so great today—but that's hardly surprising, is it?'

'Gee, thanks,' replied Donna drily.

Ally gave her an apologetic look. 'Look, what I'm trying to say is that it's *your* baby, Donna—growing inside *you*—'

'And he's the father.'

'He *impregnated* you,' said Ally, in a clipped voice. 'That's all.'

But something deep within Donna fluttered—maybe it was the baby itself, letting its own objections be known—and she shook her head. 'It isn't just a biological function,' she said quietly. 'Certainly not with Marcus. He *is* the father of this baby. In every way which counts.' She didn't know why that should be. She just knew. In the part of her that was beyond logic or reason. The part of her to which Marcus seemed to have unique access.

Ally looked torn between admiration and impatience. 'That may be,' she allowed. 'But even so, he can't just come and take it away from you—that's total male oppression!'

'Or equality,' shrugged Donna. 'Maybe men feel they've been excluded from bringing up children for long enough. That they can offer exactly the same emotional and physical sustenance as women. It all depends which way you look at it.'

'He can't just take the baby away from you,' repeated Ally grimly. 'Can he?'

Donna shook her head. 'That's the trouble. I don't know. That's something I'm going to have to find out.'

'Who from?'

'A lawyer, I guess.'

'Well, that's easy.' Ally smiled. 'Tony Paxman may not be your best friend, but he's a damned good lawyer. You told me that yourself!'

But Donna knew she couldn't go and see Tony. In fact, she couldn't face going to see anyone in Winchester. If Marcus turned this into some sort of battle it was going to be ugly. And she needed some facts at her fingertips before she cast herself in the role of local victim.

'I'm going to make a couple of phone calls,' she said to Ally. 'Can I leave the fruitcake to you?'

'Consider it done!' said Ally, with a quick glance at her watch. 'Listen, Sarah will be in soon. Why don't you take the rest of the day off?'

'Thanks, Boss!' said Donna, laughing in spite of everything.

She phoned Carly Morrison—a woman she had met years ago at an evening class, when she'd first moved to London. They had both been trying to master the art of cake decoration, and Carly had gone on to become a cookery presenter on a cable TV channel. Over the years the two of them had stayed in regular contact, and Carly had promised to come to The Buttress just as soon as her busy schedule allowed. She was unshockable, very likable—and she had lots of contacts.

Donna tracked her down to the television studios, and after Carly had demanded to know 'everything' there was to know about life running a tea-room, Donna plucked up the courage to ask her question.

'Carly, I need a favour.'

A loud, throaty laugh came ringing down the line. 'If it's a loan you're after then I'm afraid you've come to the wrong person, honey!'

'No. It's not that sort of favour. I need the name of a lawyer.'

There was a pause. 'You in some sort of trouble, Donna?'

Donna made a snap decision. If she started on her story she would never get finished, and Carly would see the pregnancy for herself soon enough. And besides, she was not going to think of this baby as anything but a joy. Certainly not trouble. 'Not at all. I just need a little advice, that's all.'

'Okay, hon—here's the number. Got a pen?'

Donna rang the number and the lawyer—who was quite clearly smitten with Carly—told her everything she needed to know.

She put the phone down slowly and went to the kitchen, to find Ally and Sarah buttering scones with the speed of women working on a production line. They both looked up as she walked in.

'Everything okay?' asked Sarah.

'I think so. I'm going to go out for a walk. I need some fresh air.'

'Donna,' said Ally warningly. 'What did the lawyer say?'

She felt light-headed. Weird. 'I'll tell you later. I must get out of here. I feel all trapped and claustrophobic.'

She saw the brief look which passed between the two of them, as if to say, I'm not surprised. They obviously thought that she was starting to feel hemmed in by the pregnancy and Marcus's threat to sue her for custody.

Outside the air was thick, the September sun beating down on her bare head like someone trying to get inside. She felt like a stranger in the place she knew better than any other. Maybe she would walk down to the market and buy herself some flowers.

She took the scenic route to the market, down through the water meadows and past the cathedral. Sweat trickled in undulating streams down her spine, and she began to wish she had worn one of the many hats she owned.

She bought two big bunches of scarlet daisies, and as she fumbled around in her purse for money she felt a slight aching at the base of her belly. Sweat broke out on her face and she saw the market trader frown.

'You all right, love?' he asked, and his voice seemed to come from a long way down a tunnel.

Donna nodded, and cradled the flowers in her arm like a baby. She would go back the shorter way. It wasn't as pretty, true, and it took her directly past Marcus's hotel, but her energy seemed to have been sapped. It was all very well telling herself that pregnancy wouldn't change anything—but for the baby's sake she was going to have to start taking things a little easier. And marching down to the market was simply asking for trouble.

* * *

Marcus was sitting in his office, drumming his fingers angrily against his desk. He had spent the last hour attempting to dictate letters to his secretary, but his words had made no sense and in the end he had grown tired of her look of surprise.

'Lets go over this again in the morning, can we?' he had growled.

'Certainly.' His secretary had given him a polite, quizzical smile. 'Er, can I fetch you some aspirin, or something, Marcus? You seem a little under the weather.'

'Nothing!' he had roared, and word had soon spread around among all the staff that Marcus was in a *filthy* temper and that no one should talk to him unless absolutely necessary.

He stared out of the window, wondering why the landscape suddenly seemed to have altered beyond his comprehension. The street was the same. The cars still moved past. So why did it all look so fundamentally different?

Because a woman was out there somewhere? he wondered. A woman who carried his child? A vulnerable woman he had threatened with litigation. He felt guilt and anger kick in, spilling around his veins in equal measures. He rested his head against the cool pane of glass and let out a sigh.

How could he have done? How *could* he? Told her that he would fight her in the courts, his very stature and determination implying that if there was a battle ahead he would be the only victor. What kind of man, he wondered, did that?

He was going to have to go and tell her that the words had been fuelled by his frustration. Not a sexual frustration—but the frustration of having set something in motion without thinking where it might lead. But maybe that was just life. People acted on impulse all the time. You could say that he and Donna had just been unlucky. He thought of her swollen belly and his heart raced. Or lucky.

He stared sightlessly at the people who ambled slowly along the pavements. Students walking in large groups, their individual uniform of jeans and T-shirts making them all look the same. Older tourists with a fortune's worth of photographic equipment dangling from around their necks. Girls in light dresses, looking no older than Donna had been that first time she had come to him looking for work.

He screwed his eyes up as one of them crossed the road. The memory could play tricks with the eyes. For a moment there that flash of bright, titian hair had jangled a distant bell of recognition, as had something in the way she walked.

But, no, that could not be Donna. It was too stooped for Donna. Donna didn't have a rounded body like the woman he was looking at.

Marcus froze.

No, of course she didn't. The Donna of his memory was young and carefree—the woman who was crossing the road was nearly a decade older and stooping beneath the burden of his child, her arms full of flowers the colour of blood.

Without thinking he reached his fist up and began to hammer on the window, and she looked up then, and saw him.

Marcus watched the emotions which flitted across her face. Surprise. Anger. And what was that...? He watched her cross back to his side of the road, her face set into a mask of grim determination.

By the time he went to meet her she was already

standing in Reception, her face as pale and as transparent as rice-paper, the blood-red flowers reflecting a sinister glow up into her colourless cheeks.

'I need to see you,' she croaked.

He took her arm, ignoring her weak attempt to shake him off. 'You need to sit down,' he corrected, and spotted his *sous chef* peering from behind a pillar. 'Graham!' he called. 'Bring tea into my office! Quickly!'

'Yes, Marcus!' said the startled chef.

Marcus guided her into his office, thinking how light she felt, boneless almost. He pulled out a chair for her, alarmed by her pallor but even more alarmed by the way she sank down into it without protest.

Donna was glad to get the weight off her feet. She released the flowers onto her lap, her palms all clammy and sticky and cold with sweat.

Marcus bent over her, his face tense. 'Donna—listen—'

'No!' She thought of the baby and that gave her strength. '*You* listen! I've spoken to a lawyer—'

'Donna—'

'Shut *up*!' she told him tiredly. 'And listen. He told me that you do not have any rights to this baby at all— not unless we are married. And as we are not married and are never likely to be—then that's the end of that!' She stared at him defiantly. 'Okay?'

He sat on the edge of his desk and watched her, recognising that she was dangerously close to tears. 'Okay,' he agreed softly.

Donna had wanted a fight. She'd wanted to storm and rage at him and… She sucked in some of the air, which seemed so still and so heavy. 'He also told me that you are able to acquire parental rights by mutual agreement.

So you need my co-operation if you want to see this baby, Marcus.'

'And if you decide not to co-operate?'

'Then you'll have to take me to court!' She paused for effect. 'And I can easily deny everything. I can tell them that someone else is the father.'

'You would do that?' he breathed.

The weight of her head seemed unbearable. 'I would do anything—*anything*—to stop you taking my child away from me, Marcus. You'd better believe that!'

He was the kind of man who needed to have every available fact at his fingertips. And he needed to know how thoroughly she had investigated the whole subject.

'What if I prove that the baby is mine?'

'And how would you do that?' she challenged. 'Certainly not by circumstantial evidence! We only had sex once, and no one has ever seen us together. It would be your word against mine!' She allowed an ironic smile to curve her lips. 'I shouldn't imagine that it would be difficult for the daughter of a stripper to convince the court that you were just one in a long line of lovers!'

His mouth tightened as he found that he couldn't bear to think of her in bed with another man. Then told himself how stupid that was.

'Of course you could always do a DNA test,' she continued. 'But the baby will have to be born first—'

'Donna, stop this right now,' he pleaded, thinking that her skin looked ashen.

'Why should I? You started it.' She locked her fingers together, as if she were about to start uttering some kind of fervent prayer. 'And when the baby is born no one will ever want to take it away—because they'll be able to see how much...' she gulped. 'How much we love one another!'

'Donna—I don't want to take your baby away from you.'

'Yes, you do!' Had he slipped a tight, iron band around her belly and tightened it without her seeing? Donna stared at him in horror, their argument completely wiped away by this new and terrifying intervention. 'Marcus?'

He saw her wince and recognised the pain and fear, sensing that something was happening now beyond both their control. 'Donna.' His voice sounded leaden. He seemed to move in slow motion towards her. He saw her stiffen, and then slump, falling forwards and knocking the daisies to the floor, their wilted scarlet petals scattering like bullets.

He heard a cry, and realised that it was his cry, not hers, because the scarlet petals had not been spilt from the broken flowers, but from the crumpled body of the woman who slid helplessly into his arms.

CHAPTER TEN

EVERYTHING was white. Clean and pure and white.

Even the light that dazzled and hurt her eyes so much that she shut them quickly, only seconds after opening them.

'Donna,' came a low, anguished voice that she knew she ought to recognise. But recognition was difficult because it didn't sound like the voice she knew at all.

'Shh. She's sleeping,' said a voice she definitely didn't recognise. 'Let her rest. She needs to rest.'

Donna heard something else. The familiar/unfamiliar voice murmuring something with an odd, broken kind of urgency. And then peace once more.

Next time she opened her eyes the light had changed. This time it was softer, more golden. Part of her wondered whether she had died and gone to heaven.

'Hello, Donna.'

This time she recognised it properly. Her lips were bone-dry, so she licked them. She blinked as she was caught in the ice-blue spotlight of his eyes, and then recoiled at what she read in them.

Pain. Harsh and unremitting pain which threw the world into sharp focus.

She remembered now. Her own pain. And blood. And Marcus looking drained, speaking urgently down the telephone. An ambulance, its siren screaming like a demented woman. The unresisting cold steel of a hospital trolley. A man in a mask. A light shining in her eyes. Pain and wetness.

'Oh, my God!' She sat bolt upright and then slumped back against the pillows. *'No!'*

He caught her and cradled her against him awkwardly, as if he was frightened to touch her. 'Wait a minute,' he whispered against her hair. 'I'll fetch the midwife.'

Midwife?

Through a sickening daze a bell sounded. Donna became aware of a dark-haired woman with dimpled cheeks who came to the other side of the bed and tried to shoo Marcus away, but he wasn't going anywhere.

The nurse wore a badge which said, 'Midwifery Sister Hindmarsh.' She looked at Donna, her dimples disappearing as she waggled her finger like a teacher. 'You're a very lucky young woman, you know, Donna.'

Donna turned her head to one side and felt a tear slide slowly down her cheek. *Lucky?* Like hell! What was lucky about being alive if you'd lost the only thing which mattered? She shook her head.

'Oh, yes, you are.' The nurse shook her head in an exaggerated manner—as if reflecting on the foolishness of pregnant young women in general and Donna in particular. 'Running around the place like that,' she tutted. 'Working yourself up into a state. Is it any wonder you had a bleed?'

Through her befuddled state something clicked in Donna's mind. The nurse was being bossy. And the nurse wouldn't dare to be bossy if…

'The baby?' she croaked.

The nurse gave a grudging nod. 'Is fine. Absolutely fine. As I said, you're a very lucky young woman.'

Not quite believing her ears, Donna turned to Marcus, a question in her eyes.

He seemed to be having some difficulty speaking, but finally he nodded. 'It's okay, Donna. It's okay.' And then he smiled—weak and watery, but definitely a smile. 'You haven't lost the baby.'

Donna tried to sit up again, but Marcus's hand seemed to be very firmly restraining her whilst at the same time managing to give her shoulderblade the most wonderful massage. If she hadn't felt so drowsy she might have swatted his hand away, but as it was she was enjoying it far too much to want him to stop.

'How long have I been here?' she whispered.

'Only a few hours. The doctor examined you and they scanned you. After that you just wanted to go to sleep—don't you remember?'

She shook her head. 'I don't really remember anything. Maybe the sleep blocked it all out.' Perhaps that was nature's way of protecting you.

'I was there when you had your scan.' His voice held an unmistakable note of pride. 'The heart was beating like crazy and the baby looks *fantastic*!' He laughed. 'Though I guess you could say I'm a little biased!'

She put her hand tentatively over her belly. It still felt big. And full. Another tear slid down her cheek.

'Don't cry, sugar,' he said softly. 'The baby's safe and you're safe. Everything's going to be all right.'

The doctor was even more forthright than the nurse had been.

'You do understand everything I've explained to you, don't you, Donna?'

Donna nodded and looked to Marcus for support, but he looked just as grim as the doctor. Actually, he looked even grimmer.

'You have a condition known as placenta praevia,' the doctor continued. 'Which means that the placenta is lying very low down in your uterus. The risk is that it will rupture and tear.' His face grew serious. 'And if that were the case, then obviously both you and the baby would be put in danger.' He gave a gentle smile. 'But as it is what we call a Grade 1 placenta praevia it is only a *small* risk, as I have already explained to your partner.'

Donna opened her mouth to explain, but when she saw the look on Marcus's face decided that it wasn't worth it. Too complicated, she thought tiredly.

'There is no need for any treatment other than rest. But you *must* rest. Do you understand that, Donna?' He turned to Marcus. 'And you must keep an eye on her. There mustn't be a repeat of what happened today. She can potter around the place, but there must be no exertion. No lifting. No riding of bicycles. And no sex!' he finished severely.

Donna had never blushed so deeply in her life. She willed Marcus to rescue her, and he did—but in a way which made her embarrassment ten times worse.

'You're talking about penetrative sex, I presume, Doctor?'

Now it was the doctor's turn to look embarrassed. 'Er, yes. Obviously—'

'And what about my business?' Donna put in hastily, because she knew that she would curl up and *die* if they said anything else on the subject.

The doctor glowered. 'Just how important *is* your baby to you, Donna?'

'More important than anything in the world,' she told him truthfully.

The doctor hid a smile. 'Good. That's all I needed to know.'

Marcus waited until she was safely strapped into his car before he reinforced what they had both heard. 'You heard what the doctor said, Donna. I hope you're going to take notice.'

Stay calm, she told herself, stay calm. She cleared her throat. 'No matter what the doctor said—I still have a business to run. I can't just pretend it doesn't exist.'

He didn't answer immediately as he manouevered the car out of the hospital gates and drove as carefully as if he had a consignment of raw eggs on the seat beside him. 'You're not to worry about the business. That's all going to be taken care of.'

Not to worry, indeed! 'But *how*, Marcus?' she wailed. 'We can't cope with just two staff and I haven't got enough money to pay someone else if I can't work myself.'

He stole a glance at her. 'Let me concentrate on the road,' he said abruptly. 'I don't want to have a row in the car.'

'Who said anything about a row?'

'That mutinous look on your face did. We'll talk about it when we get home!'

She sat back in her seat and sighed, knowing that it was pointless to argue.

But she protested when he drew up outside *his* house.

'Would you mind telling me why you've brought me here? I want to go home!'

'I know you do, but your tea-room isn't private enough,' he argued. 'And neither is the hotel. We need to talk without interruption.'

It seemed easier to agree than to protest—and besides, the sensible side of her knew he was right. So she let him lead her into the house. In fact, he actually tried to scoop her up into his arms to carry her, but she drew the line at having *that* happen. Last time he had picked

her up it had been to take her up to bed, and look where
that had led. 'Don't carry me, Marcus.'

'Why not?'

'Because I want to walk. I need to feel I can.'

'Don't you want to be cosseted?' he questioned softly.

'No, I prefer to be independent.' She smiled serenely.
'It gives a woman security—surely you know that?'

'I think I'm just beginning to find out,' he answered
wryly.

But she allowed him to settle her on a beautiful chaise
longue which stood in the bay window of the sitting
room, overlooking the garden. And she lay watching the
trees blowing gently in the breeze while Marcus went
away to make tea and sandwiches.

He sat down on a chair opposite her and waited until
she had worked her way through two rounds of egg and
cress, pleased to see her devouring the sandwiches with
that desperate kind of hunger—and the colour slowly
returning to her cheeks. His own appetite seemed to have
disappeared, along with his unshakeable belief that
whatever he wanted in life he would somehow be able
to achieve.

Because he had never felt quite so powerless as he
had done while he'd endured the long wait through the
doctor's examination. He had imagined losing the baby.
Losing Donna. The world had tipped and shifted on its
axis. It had been a sobering experience.

'Now,' he said. 'I have a proposition to put to you.'

'Go on.'

'Will you promise to hear me through without interruption?'

Donna pulled a face. 'That's a very mean request!'

'A very necessary one in your case. Will you?'

'How can I possibly answer that until I know what you're going to ask me?'

'*Please*, Donna.'

She smiled. 'I guess if you're pleading with me it must be important.'

'I'll take that as a yes.' He smiled back at her, unable to resist her at that moment and thinking what a mass of contradictions she could be. 'I know you said you didn't want to come and live here—' He held his hand up because he could see that she was itching to butt in with an objection. 'Remember what you promised!' he warned.

'But nothing has changed. I still don't want to live here.'

'Of course things have changed! You're not in a position to allow yourself the luxury of pleasing yourself. Not any more. You need to rest, Donna—you heard what the doctor said. You can't possibly go back to work. What if you wake in the night with a pain, or—God forbid—another bleed?'

'Don't!' She shuddered.

'Well, the doctor said it was unlikely—as long as you look after yourself—but it's still a possibility. You need another person around—night *and* day. If you're here I can look after you—and I should be looking after you. Hell, I *want* to look after you!'

Donna looked at him steadily. 'Finished?'

'Yes.'

'Can I speak now?'

He gave a longing kind of sigh. How could she be expecting his baby—slumped and recovering on the sofa—and yet still have the sexy air of the minx about her? 'Yes, Donna,' he said gravely. 'You can speak now.'

'Who's going to run your business for you while you're looking after me?'

'My general manager, of course.'

'*Exactly!*' She leapt on his answer with triumph. 'So who's going to run mine?'

Fortunately, he had anticipated just this question and prepared for it. 'Like I said—there's absolutely no cause for concern. I'm going to send over one of my cooks, who can help Ally with the baking. She's also prepared to wait tables if she needs to, but there are other staff I can supply, too.' He tried to tempt her a little bit more. 'To be honest, Donna, I employ a lot of people, and they are at your disposal for as long as you need them. You'll probably find that you'll be better staffed than you ever were before!'

Her face was stony. 'But you still haven't answered my question, Marcus. Who is actually going to *run* the business?'

He frowned as he tried to remember the name of the blonde who had scowled at him as if he were the devil incarnate. Was it Alison, or something? 'Ally!' he remembered. 'Or Sarah.'

'Wrong,' she corrected. 'Ally is a busy single mum with no desire to put in any more hours than she already does. And Sarah is a twenty-two-year-old with a social life which interests her more than a tea-room, not surprisingly.'

He looked at her. 'So?'

'So I'd like to know who's going to do all the ordering? Sort out rows with the laundry service? Be there to greet the tourists and generally act as host? All the unseen things which make the difference between a business running competently and running *brilliantly*. Who's going to do all that?'

Marcus could see where this was leading, and he could also see that there was only one person who could possibly do what she asked.

He sighed. 'I am, I guess.'

'Exactly! So it obviously makes far more sense for you to come and live with *me!*'

He looked at her with interest. 'How?'

'How, indeed!' she scoffed. 'You bring a suitcase and move in!'

The interest intensified. 'Maybe I should have said where?'

She looked at him steadily. 'Don't get any mistaken ideas. I may not have five bedrooms, like you—but I do have two. That's one for me and one for you. I've converted the whole upstairs into self-contained flat. You'll find all your home comforts there, Marcus. Simple.'

'Simple,' he echoed, realising this meant he would be put in the room where he had made love to her. He was about to be reminded of that afternoon every night and every morning. He sighed, and couldn't help thinking that his new accommodation was going to seem like a sophisticated form of prison.

Ally and Sarah giggled like schoolgirls when Donna broke the news to them.

'Marcus Foreman—Marcus *Foreman*—is going to be working here?' spluttered Sarah.

'Will he wear a pinny?' snorted Ally.

'Well, he could, as long as he wore it with nothing underneath,' said Sarah innocently. 'He's got the kind of body that women fantasise about!'

'Sarah!' cried Donna and Ally, in unison.

'Well, he has,' said Sarah stubbornly.

'Oh, go and make us all a cup of tea!' laughed Donna. 'And take a cold shower while you're at it!'

'So, let me get this straight,' said Ally, once Sarah had disappeared in the direction of the kitchen. 'Marcus will do everything that you usually do, and he will also provide any extra staff we need?'

'That's right. He wants to keep a close watch on me.'

'How close?'

'Ever heard of clams?'

Ally laughed. 'Oh, I see. So that means he's going to be sleeping here as well, does it?'

Donna blushed. 'There's no way round that. He thinks I shouldn't be left on my own, and even the doctor agrees about *that*. So you can stop looking at me like that, because it's not how you think!'

'Really?'

'Really! I shall have my room, and Marcus will be staying in the spare room.'

'Won't that fuel his fantasies—having you so close?'

Donna shot her an incredulous look. 'You're kidding! I don't think Marcus will be having any sexual fantasies about a woman who is beginning to resemble a mountain of lard!'

'What was that?' came an interested male voice as Marcus himself walked into the room.

Donna blushed again. 'Oh, nothing.'

'Just discussing my sexual fantasies, were you?' he enquired idly.

'If you knew, then why did you ask?'

'I just enjoy seeing you blush, Donna.'

'Well, make the most of it! Hopefully I'll become immune to your off-beat sense of humour,' she said sweetly.

'You never did before,' he smiled.

'Ah, but I was younger then!'

Ally stood up. 'Suddenly I feel a little superfluous. I think I'll go and see what's happened to that tea.'

'You don't have to,' protested Donna.

Ally smiled. 'Oh, yes, I do. You know what they say. Two's company and three in this case is most definitely a crowd!'

Ally closed the door behind her and they looked at one another across the room.

'We're going to have to avoid doing that,' said Donna.

'What? Talking about my sexual fantasies? I agree. Because life at the hotel will seem very tame by comparison if that's what counts as normal conversation over here!'

She looked into his eyes and the mischief and humour in them made a pretty potent combination.

She quickly began to straighten a stack of linen napkins. 'You know very well I didn't mean that. I was talking about excluding Ally and Sarah. And we mustn't.'

She wriggled her shoulders, as if trying to ease the tension out of them, and the fire of her hair shimmered like a beacon. Worse than that—it drew his attention to the heavy fullness of her breasts.

He felt the hot flame of desire, and dampened it down to a dull smoulder. 'You started it by talking about me while I was out of the room!'

'Eavesdroppers never hear any good about themselves,' she said serenely. 'Anyway, we were just discussing where you're going to sleep.' She smiled, and looked at the appropriately modest suitcase he had carried in with him. 'Like me to show you your room?'

'Okay.' Feeling a little like a man going off to his own execution, he followed her upstairs—noticing now how the pregnancy had added a little extra flesh to her bottom. But the added curves suited her, he decided. Maybe too much. He hadn't been upstairs since the day they'd made love, and he felt the blood heating his face as they reached the top of the stairs.

The image of that afternoon was burned indelibly into his memory, and it came on him when he least expected it or wanted it. Like when he was sitting round a table in the middle of some stuffy meeting and he would get a flashback of those pale, beautiful limbs entwined around him, or her glossy red hair spread all over the pillow.

He had convinced himself that not only was she bad for him—they were bad for each other. He had regretted that afternoon just as much as he'd revelled in its sweet, erotic memory. He had thought that not seeing her would make that memory recede and that distance would enable him to put her out of his mind—the way he had managed to do all those years before. But nothing seemed that simple any more. Nothing.

Donna saw him tense and guessed what he might be thinking—maybe because she was thinking pretty much the same thing herself. 'This is where it all started,' she observed softly as they drew up outside the spare room.

But he shook his head. 'Oh, it started long before this, Donna. It started when you walked into my hotel, dripping wet. Looking so lost and so small.'

She forced herself not to be seduced by the memory. Or his words. She led him quickly past the room which was to be his, and threw open the door of her own bedroom, and Marcus opened his eyes in surprise—as much at the room itself as the fact that she had allowed him access to it.

It was painted a soft buttermilk, with white muslin curtains billowing like clouds at the window and a snowy drift of a duvet lying like a great heap of snow on the brass bed. On the wall she had pinned different straw hats—some with flowers, some with ribbons, some battered, one scarcely worn.

'I buy a new hat every summer,' she explained, when she saw him looking at them.

'Which one did you buy this year?'

She pointed to the newest-looking one, which was decked with shiny red cherries and a scarlet ribbon. 'That one.'

'Put it on now,' he coaxed softly.

'No.'

'As the acting manager of this establishment, I command you to put it on!' he said sternly.

Funny how he could make putting a hat on seem like a highly erotic invitation. 'No, I won't! Finish looking at the rest of my room instead!'

Aching, he complied. Apart from the bed, the only piece of furniture was a dressing table—with a small stool which stood in front of it. Overall the effect was simple, clean and stylish.

She looked at him, searching his face for a reaction. 'So what do you think?'

'I like it. It's a very attractive room. Feminine without being in the least bit frilly.'

'Is it what you were expecting?'

'I don't know what I was expecting. I wasn't expecting you to come back to Winchester and start your own business.' He smiled. 'I've learnt to expect the unexpected from you, Donna—you're not an easy woman to stereotype.'

'Then let's destroy another stereotype while we're at it, shall we?' She walked over to the dressing table and picked up a photograph in a silver frame which stood among several others.

'Here.' She handed it to him.

Marcus studied it. It was of a woman aged about twenty-five. She was wearing a tiny bikini, made entirely out of silver sequins, and she stared at the camera with a smile which managed to be both saucy and innocent. Her hair was very dark, but apart from that it was easy to see the likeness—the big green eyes and the secret smile which reminded him so much of Donna's.

'It's your mother?' he guessed.

'That's right.' She pointed to the brief bikini. 'See what she's wearing?'

He nodded.

'She used to keep the bottoms on, you know. During her act. And parts of her breasts were covered by tassels. She was never completely naked.'

'You don't have to explain anything to me,' he said uncomfortably.

'Yes, Marcus, I do,' she said firmly. 'I need you to know. The word "stripper" is so emotive—but we forget how society has moved on. My mother used to wear nothing that wouldn't be worn on a beach now—or probably to a film première!' She took the photo away and put it back down. 'I'm not saying that I think it was a good job—because it wasn't. It was a lousy, stinking job. She just made it as acceptable as she could. Now look at this one—'

The next photo showed the same woman, aged about fifty. Her hair had touches of silver and she wore a simple woollen dress, a single strand of pearls at her neck. She looked, thought Marcus, like someone you would automatically give the best table in the restaurant to.

'This is some years after she bought her boarding house,' said Donna.

He couldn't keep the astonishment out of his voice. 'What happened?'

'She got herself an education. Oh, I don't mean that she started going to evening classes, or anything—just that she read books. Lots of different books. She learned how to think and she learned how to dress. She stopped believing that paste jewellery was beautiful and pearls and amber were dull. She learned the value of things.'

'But she never married again?'

'She wasn't ever married in the first place. Not to my father, anyway. I'm illegitimate,' said Donna, and gave him a wistful smile as she replaced the photo. 'You see, even that doesn't shock people any more.'

'Did it shock people when you were growing up?'

'Sometimes. But not enough to ruin my life.' She shrugged as she moved towards him. 'I'm not showing you this to get the sympathy vote, you know. My childhood made me what I am today, and I like the person I am today, so I can't regret it. Any of it.'

He reached out and captured her face, cupping it gently in the palm of his hand. 'I like the person you are today, too.'

'Well, that's a good start.'

He rubbed his thumb thoughtfully over the base of her chin. 'There are a couple of things that *you* need to know as well, Donna—and the first concerns your mother.'

She took a step back, away from the distracting feel of his thumb. 'Go on.'

'I never judged either her or you by what she did for a living—I wasn't given the opportunity. *You* were the one who assumed I was prejudiced. I objected to being lied to while you apparently trusted my brother enough to tell him everything.'

'You were always too busy. Too distracted. You put up a barrier which Lucas never did.'

'Maybe.'

'No maybe about it. It's true.' She looked at him, and realised that perhaps she hadn't been as honest as she could have been. 'I wanted you to *like* me, Marcus—not look down your nose at me. That's why I told you my mother was an actress.'

'I realise that now. Besides, I *did* like you—and the way I felt wasn't something I could control. I think I would have felt the same way if you'd told me that you'd just landed in a spacecraft from Mars!'

She looked at him. 'That was the first thing you wanted to say to me. What was the second?'

'Something I tried to tell you when you came to my office yesterday. That I never intended to fight you for custody of the baby.'

'That's what you told me.'

'I know. But I was angry. And frustrated.'

She raised her eyebrows and looked at him.

'Not in the sense that you're thinking. I meant frustrated by the whole situation, and my role as a bit-player. You were going to have my baby and I felt like I was just looking on from the sidelines.'

'I'm sorry,' she said simply, 'that one afternoon of lust—or passion, or whatever you want to call it—should have trapped you with this huge and irrevocable consequence.'

'And I'm sorry, too,' he said quietly. 'You're even more trapped by the situation than I am. It isn't your fault that the contraception failed. Anyway, there's no point in regrets. That's history—not reality. Our reality is here, and now.'

'Yes, I know.' Her words filled a silence made more intense by the realisation that he was still within touching distance.

The desire to kiss her was stronger than anything he had ever felt in his life, but now was not the right time to give in to temptation. Kisses led to inevitable conclusions. She was still pale, and fragile—no matter how much she protested to the contrary.

And the doctor had said no sex, in any case.

'Why don't you lie down and rest,' he suggested easily, 'while I go and see what needs doing downstairs?'

CHAPTER ELEVEN

FOR the first week after Marcus moved in, he and Donna walked on eggshells—behaving as politely as two people who had just met instead of two people who were soon to become parents. Somehow their lives managed to be both intimate and separate at the same time.

Marcus even went over to the hotel every morning to shower and shave, once Ally and Sarah had arrived for work. He told Donna that bathrooms were especially private places and that he wouldn't invade her space.

Donna thought he meant that her bathroom was too small—which it was—and tried not to feel offended—but she did. The same way she felt when they were sitting watching TV in the evenings, and Marcus would leap to his feet and say that he was going to do some work in the office downstairs. But he'd say it in such a growling kind of way that she found herself wondering if she had offended him.

Still, she wasn't going to find out by attempting to read his mind, and after a week she decided that they needed to talk.

She waited until Ally and Sarah had gone home after one particularly busy afternoon, and found Marcus sitting in the office, doing some paperwork of his own. His eyes looked sleep-depleted and he badly needed a shave—so how come he still looked like the most desirable man she had ever seen in her life?

He looked up as she walked in, and frowned. 'Everything okay?'

'Not really.'

He was on his feet in an instant, his face a fretwork of frowns. 'Is it the baby?'

'No, it is not the baby!' said Donna crossly. 'Every time I feel tired or have a negative thought it doesn't mean that I'm going to lose the baby!'

'Don't be so bloody flippant, Donna.'

'I'll be flippant if I like!' she retorted, knowing her voice sounded wild, but blaming it on the hormones which were raging remorselessly around her bloodstream. 'I'm the one who is actually *carrying* this child. Remember? I'm the one stuck with this bizarre situation of having you living here with me like some...some...'

'Mmm?' He raised his eyebrows, instantly on the alert. 'Some what?'

'Some...*stranger!*' she blustered.

He smiled. 'Very mild, Donna. I was expecting much worse than that!'

'*Now* who's being flippant?'

The ice-blue stare had thawed a little. 'Sit down,' he suggested softly.

Now why did Marcus suddenly sound like the host? Donna pulled out the chair opposite him and sat down.

'Tell me what you want, sugar,' he said gently.

She wondered how much she dared say, and then realised that she had nothing to lose by being honest.

'I can't see that you living here is going to work if you're just going to cook for me and bring me cups of tea all day and then hide away in another room. Like some old-fashioned retainer! Or a paying guest who isn't paying!'

'You mean you want rent from me?' he asked, deadpan.

'*No!*'

Marcus laughed. 'Okay. That's what you don't want. Now tell me what would please you.'

Donna swallowed as she studied her hands, which were neatly folded on her lap—it seemed easier that way than having to meet his eyes. He could please her just by existing. But there was being honest and being foolish, and you didn't tell a man a thing like that—especially when he hadn't shown the slightest tendency to come *near* her—let alone make love to her—in months.

She sighed. 'If you're here in body, but not in spirit, then I'm getting all the disadvantages of having someone share my house—with none of the advantages.'

'Such as?'

Donna shrugged. 'Oh, I don't know! The late-night chats over a cup of cocoa—'

'But you're not allowed late nights—remember what the doctor said?'

She pulled a face at him. 'Okay. The soul-searching, then.'

This drew a smile. 'You want to search my soul, do you, Donna?' he mocked.

'Yes, I do,' she murmured. 'If you've got one! You're the father of my baby, Marcus—and I don't want you to be a stranger to me! Or to the baby. I want to be able to answer questions about you, when he or she is older.'

The smile disappeared. 'Questions in my absence, you mean? Isn't that rather assuming that I'm not going to be around to answer them myself?'

'But that's the whole point! *I don't know!* We haven't discussed it, have we? We haven't discussed anything. How much of a hands-on father are you intending to be?' She stared at him intently. 'You can't just move in and pretend that nothing is happening. Something very big *is* happening, and we need to talk about how we're going to deal with it.'

He was silent for a moment. 'Don't you think we should take things slowly?'

'That's rich—in view of how we got ourselves into this situation in the first place! We didn't think about taking things slowly *then*! And there's a difference between taking things slowly and never getting off the starting block!'

Marcus sat back in the chair, his eyes looking very blue against the pale denim shirt he wore. 'But we can't possibly predict how we're going to react to this baby when it feels like we're making everything up as we go along. Doesn't it?' he probed.

'I guess it does.' She gave him a look which she knew was helpless, but she was past caring whether or not she appeared vulnerable. Right then she *felt* vulnerable. But she was pregnant—so she was allowed to! 'Maybe it feels like this for all parents-to-be.'

'Maybe.' He stared down at the yellow roses which stood in a crystal vase on the desk. Donna must have put them there this morning. 'What we *can* do is to make the most of the present and see where we go from there. The relationship we forge together during these next few months is going to be the foundation for the future.'

'Some foundation,' she murmured, 'when you've been actively avoiding me.'

He shook his head. 'I haven't been avoiding you, sugar. I told you. I was giving you space. Trying not to upset your life still further—'

'Marcus!' She leaned across the desk. 'About the only thing which could upset my life further at the moment would be to discover that I'm to give birth on national television!'

'Ah, yes,' he said gravely. 'I've been meaning to speak to you about that!'

Their eyes met across the desk and the sparks of humour which flew between them were unbearably erotic, Donna thought, smoothing her cotton dress down over her bump, as if to remind herself of the consequences of erotic thought.

'Tell me what you want to know,' he said.

'About you, mainly,' she said simply.

Marcus nodded, almost to himself. He'd wondered when this might be coming. He met her gaze with a mocking smile. 'I gather you don't want to hear about the highs and lows of my life as a hotelier?'

'Not really.'

'You want to hear about the other women?'

Donna drew in a sharp breath. That was what she had been hinting at, yes. She hadn't expected him to be quite so blunt about it.

He didn't wait for an answer. 'There's no need to start looking coy all of a sudden. That, presumably, is what you're angling to hear about? My past relationships?'

'I'd be lying if I told you I wasn't interested,' she told him quietly. 'Yet I'm not really certain that I want to hear about them.'

'Maybe you should start the ball rolling by telling me about yours,' he challenged softly.

'Oh, just…the usual.'

'That's a pretty sweeping definition.' He narrowed his eyes. 'Ever come close to marrying?'

'Nope. Have you?'

He shook his head. 'Never. Ever been in love?'

Well, she certainly wasn't going to admit to loving…she deliberately changed the tense…to *having* loved *him*. Honesty should not equal humiliation! 'What's love?' she asked, properly flippant this time.

'Cynic!' he laughed, but oddly he found that her answer disappointed him. Surely he wasn't so arrogant as to suppose that she had once loved him?

'Have you?' she asked him tentatively.

'Oh, there have been times in my life when I sensed that I was on the brink of something that other people might describe as love,' he said slowly. 'It's just that I always pulled back!'

'In the nick of time?' she suggested.

'Yeah. Maybe.' His eyes grew thoughtful. There *had* been women. After he'd sent Donna away, there had been quite a lot of women. As if he'd wanted to prove to himself that he was the world's greatest lover. For a time.

And in the years which had followed there had been some who'd been textbook-perfect wife material in just about every way which mattered. Yet something had always held him back from making a commitment, and he'd never come close to finding out what it was. 'Maybe,' he repeated.

The sun had moved across the sky and shadows fell onto his face, defining the dip of his cheekbones and the darkened curve of his chin. 'Now you tell me something, Donna.' He paused, searching her face for the first flicker of reaction before she had a chance to modify it. 'When you wake up each morning, there's a dreamy little interlude before reality slots into place. Right?'

'Mmm.' She narrowed her eyes, not sure what line he was going to take. 'So?'

'So when that happens, and you remember that you're going to have a baby—my baby—do you groan and turn over and feel trapped? Maybe wish it had never happened?'

Donna smiled. 'I groan, yes—always—and so would you if you woke up to raging heartburn or a feeling of nausea!'

He smiled too.

'As to whether I feel trapped.' She wriggled a bit in her seat as she gave the question some thought. 'Sometimes, obviously I do—especially when I think of the sheer commitment of having a baby. And the birth itself, of course. But I asked some of the other mothers in my antenatal group, and they said they felt exactly the same.' Her eyes softened in response to the question in his. 'As to wishing it had never happened; well, it has. Like you once said, you can't rewrite the past, but...' Her expression grew thoughtful.

'But?' He put in softly, fascinated by the dreamy look on her face.

Donna shrugged. 'It's funny, really—I mean the logical side of you thinks, Help! But then there's this soppy side of you that seems to cut right through all the practical objections. So that even though this is never how you would have planned to have a baby, you're just thinking, Oh, yes, please! I mean, it seems absolutely crazy to me—but I can't *wait*!'

'Can't you?'

'No.' She shook her head as she heard the indulgent note in his voice. 'Sad, isn't it? A psychologist would have a field-day—telling me that I was trying to create the family unit I never had myself and that's the subconscious reason why I became pregnant. Only it won't be a proper family unit at all. I'm doing exactly what my mother did, and raising a child on my own.'

He shook his head. 'Wrong, Donna. Your father deserted you, and your mother. I'm not going anywhere.'

She bit her lip, forcing herself to accept the truth, however unpalatable. 'But one day you might. One day you might not pull back from the brink. You might fall in love with a woman who will resent me—and who could blame her? If I were in her shoes I might feel the same about a casual fling who had got herself pregnant!'

'Donna,' he said patiently. 'You're accepting blame where none is due. The reason you became pregant is because the condom failed—'

'Don't!' she wailed. 'That makes it even worse. Implying that I had an "accident"—with all the negative baggage that word brings!'

'And the reason the condom failed,' he continued inexorably, ignoring her shocked gasp and her rapidly rising colour, 'was presumably because we had some of the most—' He drew a breath, not sure where this admission was going to take him. 'The *most*,' he emphasised, 'passionate sex I can ever remember.'

There was a short silence.

'Honestly?' asked Donna, her heart pumping like mad, hardly able to meet his eyes.

He noted her use of the word—a word she had used on more than one occasion today. And if he owed her anything it was that. 'Honestly,' he nodded, but then he shut up. Talking about it only made him think about it, and thinking about it didn't really help him sleep at night.

Donna tried not to read too much into his words. Just because the sex had been passionate, it didn't mean any more than that. Nor did she want it to. It was only her wildly fluctuating hormones demanding what nature had determined she should demand. A mate who would love her and provide for their child.

Well Marcus would certainly provide for their child— but that was *all* she could count on. She felt the familiar and gentle fluttering of the baby inside her, and blinked rapidly.

'Are you okay?' he demanded.

She felt oddly shy, praying that he wouldn't ask to feel—and praying that he would. 'It's the baby—it's moving!'

He was longing to touch her belly, but they had already raked up a lot of emotion today—surely any more would crowd her?

He registered all the conflicting emotions he could see on her face. There was fear and uncertainty, joy and disbelief. Heaven knew, he'd experienced them all himself, and a few more besides. 'Donna,' he said softly.

'Mmm?'

'You look tired.'

'I am a bit.'

'Right, then,' he said briskly. 'Go and lie down before dinner.' He saw her expression and knew what it meant. 'And stop worrying. I won't be the unpaying guest any more. Everything will be exactly as you want it to be— you only have to say. In the evening we will talk to your heart's content.' He smiled. 'Do you still play cards?'

'I'm a little rusty.'

'I could give myself a handicap.'

'That would be very sweet of you,' said Donna innocently. 'I'm sure I'd never manage to beat you these days.'

CHAPTER TWELVE

'SO WHAT do you want to do tonight, sugar?'

Donna looked up from her tapestry as Marcus breezed into the sitting room. She was embroidering a snow-white goose with a big blue ribbon around its neck. For the baby.

She'd never thought she would be the kind of person to enjoy precision sewing, but to her suprise she not only loved it, but was good at it, too. It was the perfect occupation for someone who wanted to be doing something but wasn't allowed to move much! And at this late stage in her pregnancy she physically *couldn't* have moved much—even if the doctors had told her she could!

She gave a dreamy sort of smile as she gazed up at him. 'Shall we play cards?'

Marcus pulled a face, and moved around the room restlessly. 'I'm bored with cards.'

'You're just fed up with losing!'

'I only let you win because of your delicate condition!'

'Of course you do!' Donna bit back a smile. 'Anyway, I don't feel in the least bit delicate at the moment.'

'No.' He ran his eyes over her. 'You don't look it, either. You look as healthy as an—'

'Ox?' she supplied drily.

'That wouldn't have been my first word of choice, no.'

'How about—like a barrage balloon?'

157

He considered this, relishing the invitation for him to look at her properly. Normally he had to do it when she wasn't aware he was watching her. Like when she was asleep. And at thirty-seven weeks into her pregnancy she was sleeping a lot. Then he would feast his eyes on her burgeoning figure with a mixture of pride and lust.

Especially lust.

He'd always found Donna sexually attractive, but it had come as a revelation for him to discover that he found her just as desirable when she was almost full-term with the baby.

Almost as big a revelation as discovering that he *could* reign in his sexual desire for her when he needed to. It hadn't been easy, but over the past few months—somehow—he'd kept the pleasurable, persistent ache of longing well hidden from her.

'Er, no.' He swallowed. 'You don't look like a barrage balloon, either.'

'What then?'

It was that slumberous little side glance that played such havoc with his composure! 'Just stop playing the tease, will you, Donna?' he growled. 'Or you might find you get more than you bargained for!'

Donna looked up at him thoughtfully as she leaned back against the bank of cushions, thinking how disgustingly healthy and vibrant and sexy he looked in a charcoal sweater and dark cords. But he looked distinctly grumpy, too—and just when she had thought that things between them were ticking along so beautifully.

In one corner of the room over by the window stood the Christmas tree which Marcus had dressed the day before—although she had masterminded all decorations from her almost permanant position on the sofa!

It was hard to believe that he had been sharing her

flat for over three months—yet he had slotted into her life as though he had been born for just that purpose. What was even harder to believe was that their baby would be born soon after the month was out. But Donna wasn't scared; she just wanted the waiting to be over.

'You're very jittery tonight,' she observed, in that calm, almost sleepy manner which seemed to be part and parcel of being pregnant.

'Yeah, well.' He scowled.

'Well, what?'

He shook his head. 'Nothing.'

'Marcus,' she said patiently. 'You can't come out with elusive little snippets like that and then not explain yourself. What's troubling you?'

He studied her carefully. 'You are—or rather, your attitude is.'

'Oh? You don't like the way I overrode your opinion on the tinsel?' she suggested lightly, looking in the direction of the Christmas tree, because anything was better than meeting that sizzling blue stare which was making her feel all mushy inside. 'Or do you think we've gone over the top with the angel hair?'

'Hell, Donna!' he exploded. 'That illustrates my point exactly!'

'What does?'

'You take things so lightly.'

She *did* meet his gaze then, and her expression was fierce. 'Are you suggesting that I'm not taking this pregnancy seriously?'

'Yes! *No!* Oh, I don't know!'

'Tell me,' she coaxed.

He ran his hand distractedly through the ruffled dark hair and flopped down onto a chair. 'Physically, you're doing everything the doctors and the midwife tell you—'

'Sounds like there's a "but" coming,' observed Donna drily.

'But I don't know anything about your mental state!'

Donna blinked. 'You think I'm crazy—is that it?'

'Donna!'

'Well, that's what it sounded like!'

'You never tell me about your worries!' he said stubbornly. 'Your doubts, your fears, your uncertainties!'

'You're assuming I've got some?'

'I know you have.'

Donna looked at him steadily. 'Oh? How?'

'Remember September?' he asked.

'That was months ago!'

'I don't need a speaking calendar! I know when it was,' he told her waspishly. 'Remember we were walking back from the cathedral and you saw that whole bunch of schoolchildren?'

The children had been noisy and laughing and wearing uniforms which had looked much too big for them. 'Yes. I remember. What about it?'

'And you went all quiet, didn't you? I saw you looking at one child in particular.'

A child with eyes that had reminded her so much of *his* eyes. 'Yes.'

'And I knew you were trying to imagine *our* child going to school like that—'

'Only I couldn't,' she put in quietly. 'It seemed too far in the future. Too impossible to imagine. Anyway...' She smoothed her hand down over her swollen belly. 'While I'm flattered that you noticed my reaction, that *was* three months ago. Why did it take you so long to get around to asking me, Marcus?'

He gave a sigh. 'Because when the doctor told you to take it easy, I sort of assumed that meant pushing the more awkward issues to one side. I didn't want it to come over as a criticism of *you*.'

'And wasn't it?'

He shook his head. 'Not at all. Surely it's only healthy to be aware of the difficulties which lie ahead of us? If you thought that everything was going to be one hundred per cent perfect for one hundred per cent of the time, then I *would* be worried. Because that would be unrealistic.' There was a brief pause, and his eyes took on an almost luminous intensity. 'Any regrets, Donna?'

She went very still. 'Have you?'

He gave a faint smile. 'That isn't fair.'

'Tell me what *is* fair.' She smiled, but the question in her eyes did not go away.

Marcus hesitated. Analysing how he felt still seemed pretty alien to him—but he owed Donna the truth. Hell, he owed her a lot more than that, but truth came pretty high up the list.

'I did have a few regrets,' he admitted. 'Right at the beginning.'

Donna nodded, respecting the honesty which lay behind his answer and realising how much simpler it would have been for him to have lied to her. 'But not any more?'

He shook his head. 'Now I just want it to happen. Sometimes it seems as though it never will. And sometimes I try to imagine what things will be like when the baby arrives, but I just can't. It's too big.' He stretched his legs out and gave her a lazy smile. 'But then I could never have imagined living with you, like this—'

'And finding it tolerable?' she questioned casually.

'Finding it more than tolerable!' he teased. 'Finding that I like it very much.' Apart from the fact that sexually she was off-limits, of course. And he wouldn't dream of telling her *that*. His face grew serious. 'I just want more than anything for the two of you to be safe and healthy.'

Donna nodded. 'I know you do.' With her finger she traced a line around the circumferance of her bump. 'It's funny—we've been to all the classes and read all the books; I've eaten the right things and done everything I've been told to—but there's still this great sense of uncertainty—of leaping into the unknown. That *is* scary—but then, life *is* scary sometimes.'

He nodded, finding the sight of her swollen body unbearably moving. He thought how brave she had been. She'd never complained of tiredness, or of losing her figure as he knew so many women did. 'Whatever happens between us, Donna,' he said suddenly, 'we have to make things work for the baby's sake.'

It sounded awfully as if he was preparing her for the inevitable—and in Donna's eyes the inevitable was that Marcus would move out as soon as the baby was born. And that she would only see him when he came round to collect the child. She pushed the image away. 'Yes,' she agreed. 'I know we do.'

'Both of us had crazy childhoods, sugar—let's make sure we don't pass the same legacy onto our baby.'

Her smile wasn't as steady as she would have liked, but that wasn't really surprising when he said our baby like that. It was such an emotional phrase to use.

He saw her look of uncertainty and wanted to take her in his arms there and then, but he was terrified that she would misinterpret the gesture. And besides, he wasn't sure that he trusted himself to. Self-control was one thing, but the strain of living so closely with her and not being permitted to lay a finger on her was beginning to tell. He didn't know how she did it, but her inbuilt sensuality seemed to have grown along with the baby—and he would defy any normal, red-blooded male not to have felt the same as he did.

Not that they had been doing anything likely to fan the flames of passion—quite the opposite, in fact. They spent long lazy evenings and weekends together. Marcus cooked and Donna continued to eat enough for two—sometimes three. They played cards and watched television—though the channel was swiftly changed if there was anything on it which was even *remotely* connected to sex.

They read books—sometimes they even read the same books and then they discussed them afterwards. Sometimes the discussions were amicable, when they agreed on something. More often than not they could only have been descibed as 'heated'.

And heated was also the only way he could describe the way she left him feeling most evenings when she demurely went to bed—at some unholy hour. Sometimes as early as nine o'clock! He would try to concentrate on something other than how soft and pale and beautiful and *lonely* she must be feeling, upstairs underneath that snowy-white duvet. While he sat alone, mocked by memories.

'Are you hungry?' he asked her, with a gentle smile.

'Not really.' She lay back against the cushions and clasped her hands over her belly. 'It doesn't feel as if there's very much room in there tonight. Certainly not for food. Ouch!'

Marcus brightened. 'Baby moving?'

'Baby making attempt on prenatal kick-boxing championship, more like!'

'Can I feel?'

There was barely a flicker of hesitation before she

said, 'Of course.' She had never said no to him before, but then he hardly ever asked, even though she sensed he was dying to feel his child moving. She suspected that he found it just as difficult and distracting as she did.

She sat up a little straighter and shifted up the sofa to make way for him, dreading the feel of his warm hand on her belly. Well, not dreading it so much as wondering whether she would manage to sit through it without wriggling—but then it was such an intimate thing to do, when you thought about it.

He nestled up close and gently put the flat of his hand down on her belly, and almost immediately the baby aimed a healthy kick at it.

'Ouch!' He retracted the hand in mock-pain. 'I can see what you mean! Donna, it must hurt like hell.'

She shook her head. 'No, it doesn't. It's a funny, fantastic feeling. I can't really describe it.'

'Look!' he exclaimed, and bent his dark head to study the bump intently. 'You can see the shape of the heel quite clearly. Look—it's like a fish moving around underneath the surface!'

He sounded as excited as a little boy whose favourite team had just won the league! Donna smiled. 'A fish? More like a dolphin!'

He put his hand back over her umbilicus and just let it rest there, then turned his head to look at her. 'Do you think it's a boy?'

'Yes,' she nodded. 'Or a girl!'

'Donna!'

'Marcus!' she teased.

'Do you wish we'd found out?'

During one of her routine scans they had been asked whether they wished to know the sex of their child, and they had looked at one another and shaken their heads at exactly the same time and said, 'No thanks.'

'No, I don't,' said Donna. 'I want there to be a nice surprise at the end of all that labour!'

His heart leapt with anxiety. 'I wish I could do it all for you, sugar.'

'Well, you can't. You're not biologically programmed to!' She snuggled back comfortably against the cushions. 'But it's sweet of you to say so.'

He wondered if she was as aware as he was that his fingers were within touching distance of her breasts, which had been growing bigger by the day. He ached to touch them.

She was wearing a maternity dress that he had bought for her in London. He had travelled up for a meeting—very reluctantly—and only after making water-tight arrangements ensuring that Donna would be well looked after. He had been heading for the Tube, walking down one of those fancy streets in the centre of the city, when he had seen the maternity shop.

He had wandered in without really knowing what he wanted. If anything. But there had been several very helpful sales assistants who had fussed around him as if he were the first father since the world began. They'd asked what colour hair Donna had. And what colour eyes. And they'd complimented him on his descriptive powers, claiming that most men didn't have a clue what colour their wives' eyes were! And he hadn't corrected them.

He had ended up buying a knee-length velvet dress—the pale green colour of a new leaf, expensive and highly impractical. It was fitted on the bust, from where it fell in softly draped folds to just above the knee, showing off her magnificent legs. He thought it made her look like some contemporary Grecian goddess.

'That dress looks wonderful,' he said in a throaty voice.

'Does it?'

'Mmm. You look like a green bud, about to burst into leaf.'

'It's far too good to be wearing round the house like this, but I keep thinking that there are only three weeks to go—so I'd better get as much wear as I can from it.'

'Mmm,' he said again, hardly hearing a word she said, aware only of his child growing deep inside her.

Donna realised that his hand was still lying over her stomach, and she would have moved except that he seemed so contented like that, and to be truthful—she *liked* it. She felt safe. Protected.

Marcus held his breath. He had been expecting her to shift uncomfortably away from him, but he felt no resistance—not even passive resistance. Through the soft green material of her dress he could feel the baby—not belting its limbs around any more, but obviously just squirming around happily.

Donna relaxed. Why not just lie back and enjoy what was a perfectly relaxed and conventional pose between two parents-to-be? Okay—they might be not be the most conventional *couple* in the world, but so what?

She liked the gentle pressure of his hand. In fact she felt so comfortable that she might even think about resting her head on his shoulder. And why not? They had already agreed that he would be present at the birth—and you couldn't get more intimate than *that*.

Marcus's pulse rocketed as he felt her relax against him. It was pitiful! Laughable, really—that such a small crumb of affection should bring him such pleasure. And even more laughable that he should suddenly feel like a complete novice. Except that he *was* a complete novice in this situation. He had never made love to a pregnant woman before...

And you're not going to make love to one now, he told himself firmly. All she's doing is resting her head on your shoulder!

Donna closed her eyes and felt herself drifting into a place somewhere between wakefulness and sleep. Where sight and sound retreated to a distant place, and where sensation overwhelmed everything else. She could feel the weight of the baby, and its occasional bubbling little movements. She snuggled into the hard contour of Marcus's shoulder, and felt the firm flesh and the whispering of silk as his shirt brushed against her cheek. She sighed.

Unable to resist any longer, Marcus let his thumb brush lightly against the base of her swollen breast, and held his breath while he waited for her reaction. But she just sighed again.

This time the touch of his thumb was more deliberate, and this time the breath which escaped her sounded deliciously dreamy. He grew bolder. Drew slow, light circles round and round the nipple until he felt her moving impatiently beneath him, making a protesting little cry.

'Donna?' he said softly.

She opened her eyes to find him watching her. 'Mmm?'

'Did I wake you?'

'I wasn't asleep.'

'Were you pretending to be?' he asked suddenly.

She felt lazy and comfortable, the blood pulsing through her veins like honey. 'Yes. Naughty of me, wasn't it?'

'Why bother pretending?'

The baby was impeding her ability to shrug. 'I suppose I thought that if I pretended, then I could just lie back and enjoy what you were doing. Without having to question whether I should be letting you.'

'Don't feel guilty,' he urged.

'It's easy for you to say that. Men don't seem to have the same hang-ups about sex...as women.' She had very nearly said sex without love.

'Don't have hang-ups. Just enjoy it.'

'Mmm.' She was keeping her eyes open only with the greatest of concentration. 'What's the matter, Marcus? I've never seen you looking so edgy before.'

Because he had spent every day and every night under her roof in a state of near-permanant excitement, while he behaved in the most decent way he knew how. Knowing that he couldn't—no, *mustn't* go near her. If it had been anyone else he might have tried, but not Donna. Not after the urgent way they had fallen into bed last time. And she was pregnant—so he had all the protective baggage which went with that.

It was just that the thought that maybe she'd wanted him to do this to her all along was nearly driving him out of his head with excitement. 'I thought you were about to leap up and slap me around the face.'

'I don't think I could leap anywhere at the moment,' she said drily.

'Oh.' He recognised the husky note in her voice. She wanted him to carry on—he would have staked everything he owned on that. 'Well, maybe I should just continue with what I was doing,' he said thickly. 'Who knows? It might even send you to sleep.'

'I suppose it might,' she agreed unconvincingly, and she lay back and closed her eyes again.

He was almost frightened to begin, for fear that he would never be able to stop. And he must be able to stop. The slightest hint of resistance or second thoughts on Donna's part and he would put an end to it without her having to utter a word.

His whole hand cupped her breast while the thumb began to tease the swollen, tightened centre. He watched the unconscious way her body communicated its pleasure to him. Her lips were parted and her breath beginning to quicken. He watched the way her head tipped back, as if its weight was too great a burden for the pale column of her neck and that great heavy rope of hair hanging down her back. He noticed the slow unfurling of her fingers, like petals warming to the sun. And he knew that if her eyes were open the pupils would be huge and black and dilated.

He idly changed the direction of his thumb and heard her purr with pleasure in response, and it was only then that he bent his head and began to kiss her.

'Oh,' she sighed with longing against his mouth. She just couldn't stop herself. Only a self-deluding fool would claim that she hadn't wanted him to do this for days. Weeks. Months, even.

He smiled into her lips. 'I could kiss you all night.'

Her eyes flickered open. 'I might even let you.'

'Really?' he murmured.

'Mmm. Really.' Donna had thought that he would immediately start removing her clothes, but he didn't. Instead, his hand went to the band which was tied tightly around her plaited hair, and he pulled it free. Unravelled the emerald velvet ribbon woven into the strands until her hair hung in crude ringlets around her face.

'Shake your head,' he whispered.

She did as he asked and her hair erupted and casaded like amber around her shoulders.

'You're my fantasy come to life, Donna. Do you know that?'

No, *you're* the fantasy, she thought. You're *my* fantasy come to life. And I love you.

His hand began to sculpt her body from breast to thigh, over and over again, until she felt weak with wanting. And then he carefully rucked the velvet dress up to her waist, exposing her vast belly in the tent-sized knickers. She drew her knees up immediately.

'Don't,' she objected.

'Don't what?'

'Don't even look at me.'

'But you're beautiful.'

'No, I'm—'

'Yes,' he contradicted, and traced a lazy line across the drum-tight bump, and it seemed like the most arousing gesture he had ever made. 'Big and proud and beautifully ripened.'

She gave up fighting and let him slide his hands round to cup the firm jut of her buttocks. Let him kiss her eyelids, the tip of her nose and the corners of her mouth. She felt the light touch as his fingers feathered her where she was warm and moist and aching—until she was lost in a dark, erotic world of his creation. She said his name, just once, and then began to move distractedly beneath his touch.

Marcus looked down at her while he continued to caress her, revelling in the frantic little movements of her limbs. He knew it would be more practical to take her upstairs, but he could also see that she was close to the edge. Too close. And too precious and unwieldy to just fling over his shoulder and mount the stairs and take her upstairs to bed.

Which meant staying right here...

He slid his hand inside her panties and she made an agitated little sound that was somewhere between a gasp and a cry as he moved his hand against her heated flesh with a slow, sure rhythm.

This was all going to be over far too quickly, was his one regretful thought as he watched the frantic circling of her hips.

Donna felt the first spasm of pleasure ripple with increasing strength through her body, on and on and on, until she thought she would die with pleasure or astonishment. Or both. She called his name out loud. And then she cried.

He took her upstairs and undressed her like a child, finding a nightdress tucked underneath her pillow and pulling it over her head. It was made of fine white lawn—all tucked and embroidered—and with the thick red hair falling in a bright mane over her breasts she looked impossibly flushed and sexy and beautiful.

She was all sleepy as he pulled the duvet over her, and his body felt dry and aching, and he knew that if he didn't get out of here soon...

He was just tiptoeing out when her voice halted him.

'Marcus?'

He turned around.

Her eyes were wide open. 'Come to bed.'

He shook his head. 'You're tired now and you need to sleep. It doesn't matter,' he lied.

'Yes, it does. I want to hold you. I want you to hold me.'

'What if I said no?'

'You want to make me clamber out and chase you? In my condition?' she mocked.

He smiled. 'Well, I've tried to do the gentlemanly thing.'

'And I'm not going to let you.'

'Oh, well, in that case…' His eyes narrowed like a cat's as he shut the door softly behind him and began to unbutton his shirt.

He was tempted to tear the garment from his body in his eagerness to fall into bed with her, but he didn't want to frighten her. So he made his undressing as unhurried as he could and saw that she was watching the slow striptease through lazy, slitted eyes, clearly enjoying it. And by the time he slipped underneath the sheets to join her, he discovered that she was trembling nearly as much as he was.

She wrapped her arms almost shyly around his neck. 'I'm going to make love to you now.'

He shook his head. 'No, sugar. The baby. Remember what the doctor said. No sex.'

'But there are other ways. Aren't there?'

'There sure are.'

'I want to pleasure you the way you did to me,' she whispered. 'Will you show me how?'

Her innocent question caught him by surprise. So did the trusting way she asked it. Did that mean what he thought it might mean? But then the throb of anticipation blotted out the question. 'You bet your life I will,' he murmured. Marcus took her hand and softly kissed each finger in turn, then the palm. Only then did he let his body relax with anticipation against the mattress as he held her by the waist. 'Lesson number one…' his voice was soft '…you bend your head and you kiss me.'

CHAPTER THIRTEEN

DONNA woke him some time in the night.

'Marcus!' she hissed urgently, shaking his shoulder. 'I think I felt something!'

Lost in the memory of one of the most beautiful orgasms of his life, Marcus felt himself stir. 'Mmm. So did I!'

'I'm serious!'

Moving swiftly out of the memory, he sat up in bed his eyes snapping open. 'You mean it's the baby?'

'I'm not sure.'

He frowned. 'It can't be! There's still another three weeks to go.'

'It could be. Babies come early.'

'Keep still, then.' He slid his arms around her shoulders and cuddled her against him, loving the feel of her bulky stomach pressed up this close to him. 'And we'll wait and see.' He gave the top of her head a perfunctory kiss. 'Okay?'

'Okay.'

They both held their breath almost without realising they were doing so, then let it out in unison as nothing happened.

He stroked her hair and slid a hair-roughened thigh over hers. 'I guess we just wait. I can't think of a nicer way to do it.'

'Me, neither.' She nestled against his bare chest, so comfortable in his arms.

Marcus lay in silence for a moment, just listening to

the sounds of the evening—the ticking of a clock in the room and the distant hum of a car outside. There were things he wanted to ask her, but he wondered if now was the right time. Maybe there never would be a right time.

'What is it?' she murmured sleepily against his chest.

'How do you know it's anything?' He smiled in the darkness.

'You tensed up your shoulders—the way you always do when you want to ask a difficult question.'

He thought about this. 'You know me pretty well now, don't you, Donna?'

Donna felt protected by the cloak of darkness, and secure enough to say what was on her mind. 'I think I always have done. Only I never felt your equal before.'

'But you do now?'

'Oh, yes.'

He took a deep breath, but before he could speak she said it for him.

'You want to know if you're the only lover I've ever had, don't you, Marcus?'

He was stunned by her perception, even if he had already worked out the answer for himself. 'I have no right to ask.'

'Yes, you do. There shouldn't be any no-go areas of knowledge. Only you have to be prepared to hear things you might prefer not to.'

He sighed. 'It was a naive and unrealistic expectation.'

Donna smiled. 'Yes, it was, but so what? We all have them—or did you think that as a man you were immune? I wish you'd never had any other woman than me, but you have.'

'Yes, I have.' He paused. 'But what if I told you that no woman has ever come anywhere close to affecting me the way you do? On any level.'

'And what if I told you that there has only ever been one other man—'

'And did he love you?'

'Yes. Very much.'

'But you didn't feel the same way?'

'No,' she answered quietly, thinking, How could she have done—when she had only ever loved Marcus? She forced her thoughts away from the wishful to the practical. 'You know, we still haven't talked about what's going to happen after the birth.'

'Because we agreed we wouldn't try to predict the future. Especially not about the important things.'

'And what are the important things? The baby is going to be born soon—maybe sooner than either of us think. Surely we're close enough to the future now for me to ask you a question like that.'

He scowled, knowing now another reason why they had always avoided the subject. Too painful. 'Well, most important to me is how often I get to see the baby, I guess.'

'You mean access arrangements?'

Marcus nodded, wincing in the darkness at the coldness of the phrase. 'We can have a lawyer draw up some kind of formal agreement, if you'd prefer.'

Donna took her head from his chest and leaned over him, even though she could only see the smoky gleam of his eyes in the dim light. 'Is that what you want?'

He laughed, only it didn't sound bubbling, or humorous. 'I don't think what I want is relevant.'

'Of course it is!' she said fiercely. 'You're the father!'

'But only the biological father!' he snarled.

'What other kind is there?'

'The real kind! The kind that wipes his nose when he gets a cold. Or kicks a ball around in the park with him.

The kind that shows him how to ride a bike without falling off and how to deal with bullies when they pick on you!'

'And what if we have a girl?' asked Donna primly.

'Exactly the same!' He scowled. 'And don't try to be clever *or* change the subject, Donna King! You blithely talk about what it would be like if I met another woman—don't you ever give a thought to what it would be like for me if *you* met another man? Will I have to stand and watch from the sidelines while he or *she*,' he corrected hurriedly, 'calls another man Daddy? I don't think I could stand it,' he finished ferociously.

'Why are we arguing about a mythical man I might never meet at a time like this?' she asked him. 'I thought we had had just enjoyed a mutually satisfactory experience—'

He sighed. 'That's just the problem. We have.'

'And? How is that a problem?'

'It makes me realise how much I…want you.' It didn't seem quite the right word, but it would do for now. 'I want you even more now than ever before, Donna. If anything, the sex has only made things worse—it's made me realise what I've been missing!'

He was right—the sex had changed everything. Donna had a sneaking suspicion that sometimes men's minds and women's minds were heading in the same direction—only taking two entirely different routes to get there. She loved him. She knew that. She thought that deep down he felt the same way about her. But she wasn't going to put words in his mouth, however much she wanted to hear them.

'You mean you want to start having sex regularly?' she asked casually.

Marcus snapped the light on, and through the blinking

of her eyes in reaction Donna saw him glaring at her as though she had just uttered the most awful blasphemy. *'No!'* he roared.

Donna pretended surprise. 'You don't want sex?'

'Yes!'

'Marcus, if you're going to yell like a hooligan then I suggest you go back to your own room!'

'If you weren't pregnant I'd put you over my knee!' he retorted.

'If I weren't pregnant, then you wouldn't *be* here, buddy!'

'Says who?'

'Says me!'

'Oh, yes, I would!' he said fervently.

There was a pause. 'You would?' Donna gulped.

'Of course I would! Because sooner or later I would have come to my senses and realised just how much I love you. And I do, Donna. I love you very much.'

She gazed back at him, too scared to hope for what had always seemed like an unobtainable dream. He'd said the words, and she believed that he meant them—but was there substance behind them? Enough to withstand all the tests that life threw in the path of love?

She thought how easy they were in each other's company—just as they had been all those years ago. They laughed at the same jokes, they disagreed on all the things that men and women had been disagreeing on for years. Like whether women could read maps or men could do more than one task at a time.

She didn't have much experience of the opposite sex, but she knew that whatever chemistry they had in bed was pure magic.

So did that add up to love?

'I love you, Donna,' he repeated softly, and cradled

her tenderly against him. 'If I hadn't been so damned dense I might have admitted it to myself a whole lot sooner.'

Her heart filled with a feeling of contentment so pure that it made her feel quite dizzy. 'I love you, too.' She turned to rest her head against his chest, and sighed. 'Oh, Marcus!'

He stroked her arm. 'Mmm?'

'This is what it could have been like—if only we'd stayed together.'

He shook his head, secure now, letting go of the last of his regrets. 'No, sugar,' he said softly. 'We were both too young—the gulf was too wide. I was too arrogant and you were too...'

'Too what?'

'Too good for me!' he said fiercely.

Donna smiled and didn't correct him. After all, it didn't do a man any harm to have respect for the woman in his life!

'We needed to part in order to grow, and—'

'Marcus!' she interrupted frantically.

'What?'

Donna gasped, and this time she looked scared. 'It's the baby,' she told him, wide-eyed. 'It's coming!'

'How do you know?'

'I just know,' she said firmly, as women had been saying to their men since time began.

The journey to the hospital seemed to take for ever.

Marcus had never felt so helpless in his life as he'd located his car keys with shaking fingers. He had briefly considered calling an ambulance, but decided that the journey would be faster and more reliable if he was in the driving seat.

Which meant that now all his attention was taken up with trying to steer the car as smoothly as possible, with his precious cargo sitting in the passenger seat beside him. It meant that he wasn't able to touch Donna, or to comfort her. He was forced to concentrate on the road—and he didn't need to keep looking at her to know that she was suffering. Her eyes were huge and dark in a snowy-white face as the contractions started coming more frequently and more powerfully.

He saw her stiffen as another spasm passed, and he glanced over at the illuminated clock on the dashboard.

'How often are they coming now?' she croaked.

'About every five minutes.'

'That's quick. I think. *Oh!*' She clung onto her belly.

'Donna, I can't bear to see you this way,' he moaned, as she gave a sudden whimper of distress. 'What can I *do* for you, sugar?'

'Just keep driving.'

'Do you think—'

'No, I don't! I'm not thinking about anything—and neither should you if you're going to fret! If you want something to take your mind off things, Marcus, then try deciding what baby names you could live with, as that's something else we didn't get around to deciding!'

Things got a little better when they arrived at the hospital. At least there were people in uniform who seemed to know what they were doing. For once in his life Marcus was happy to stand on the sidelines and let them take over, while Donna was bundled onto a trolley and rushed up to the labour ward.

'Just grip my hand,' Marcus urged her as they waited for the lift, not seeming to notice that her nails were making tiny red, crescent-shaped lacerations on his palms.

Donna had shut her eyes now, as if to blot out the pain, and he saw her face contort against the force of the new life trying to push its way out of her body. He found himself wishing that he'd told her he loved her sooner. Or maybe wishing that he hadn't been so damned arrogant in the first place, and then they would never have been in this situation.

But he wouldn't have unwished that. Not for the world. Because hand in hand with his natural fears for Donna and their baby came the most breathless excitement he had ever felt. As if a miracle was happening right now and right here. And he was part of it.

The midwife who admitted her onto the labour ward was Sister Hindmarsh—the same rather bossy nurse who had given Donna such a stern lecture when she had been taken there with the bleed, all those months ago. But now her face was wreathed in smiles as Donna was wheeled into the delivery room.

'Hello again, my dear!' she beamed. 'I was rather hoping I might be on duty when you came back!'

'Nurse, I need to push!' moaned Donna.

'Well, you *think* you do, dear,' said the midwife kindly, clearly not believing a word of it. 'That's what all you first-time mothers say—but because it's a first baby, I think you'll find you've got a lot longer to wait than that! Now, let's have a quick look at you...' She lifted up Donna's gown and her face underwent a startling transformation. 'Oh, good heavens!' she exclaimed. 'You're fully dilated!'

'Is that bad?' demanded Marcus.

'No, it's wonderful,' answered the midwife. 'It means we're going to have a baby! And sooner, rather than later!'

'Marcus!' Donna's voice cracked as she gripped onto

his hand, her body tensing up to face the next contraction. 'Please don't leave me.'

'I'm not going anywhere, sugar!'

Marcus had never known an experience as powerful as seeing his child being born—but along with the pride came panic. He tried telling himself that women had been giving birth for centuries, in conditions far more threatening than the clean and antiseptic surroundings of this hospital delivery room.

But nothing seemed to take the edge off his fears for Donna and their baby.

Nothing, that was, until Donna gave one last shuddering groan—and a long, skinny object with a shock of dark hair emerged, shouting, into the world.

'It's a boy!' beamed the midwife, over the baby's first lusty scream. 'A beautiful baby boy.' She creased her brows as she deftly delivered the child onto Donna's stomach. 'And just about the longest-looking baby *I've* ever seen. He'll be tall—'

'Just like his father,' said Donna breathlessly, and smiled up into Marcus's eyes.

'And would you like to cut the cord, Mr King?' asked the midwife.

Marcus would have said that he was one of life's more confident men, but he knew he would rather risk bungee-jumping from the top of the tallest skyscraper than risk harming his baby son. 'I'd rather leave it to the experts,' he answered with a tight smile. 'And the name is Foreman.'

'Oh. Is it?' said the midwife, with studied casualness, and something in her tone made Marcus look up at her with a puzzled frown.

The cord dealt with, the midwife latched the baby onto Donna's breast. 'I normally go and make you both a cup of tea now,' she explained. 'Gives you a couple of quiet minutes alone with your baby.'

Once she had gone, the delivery room was filled with the sound of contented glugging, and their eyes met with delight and disbelief over the small dark head.

'He's here,' said Donna. 'And somehow it feels as though he was always meant to be.'

Marcus swallowed as he bent to wipe a damp strand of hair away from her forehead, and he was overwhelmed with a love so pure that he vowed never to forget the way he felt right at that moment. 'Thank you, Donna,' he said simply.

'You're welcome!' She looked up and her eyes were shining. 'Isn't he beautiful?'

'He sure is. As beautiful as his mother.'

'No. Much *more* beautiful!' she insisted, confidently moving the baby onto the other breast while Marcus watched with wondering eyes.

'Where ever did you learn to do that?'

'I didn't,' said Donna, with a slow smile. 'I just knew he was finished on that side. And we're going to have to choose a name for him soon—I can't keep saying "he" and "him" the whole time! Did you have any ideas in the car?'

Marcus shrugged. 'Sort of. You say first.'

'Well, I quite like Nick.' Donna stroked the downy head. 'Your father was Nick, and my mother's middle name was Nicola, and I thought...'

Her train of thought was interrupted by the return of Sister Hindmarsh, who was looking at Marcus with a definite question in her eyes. 'So. Have you come to any decisions yet?'

Marcus smiled. 'Not quite. Though we both like the name Nick.'

The midwife threw him one of her despairing looks. 'Mr Foreman!' she exclaimed. 'Have you not asked this poor girl to marry you yet?'

The pale blue eyes lit up with amusement as he met Donna's eyes. 'Well, she might not agree to have me.'

The midwife gave a loud sigh which was obviously meant to signify her disapproval of false modesty.

'Will you marry me, sugar?' he asked softly.

Donna was tempted to giggle with sheer happiness as Nick's mouth slid sleepily from the nipple. 'Marcus, you don't have to marry me just for the baby's sake—'

'But I'm not!' he put in quickly. 'I want to marry you because I love you. More than words could ever say. I was intending to ask you earlier, but we...I...' He grinned and shrugged helplessly. 'Fell asleep.'

'Marcus!' she murmured, on a half-hearted note of protest.

He crouched down beside the bed, so that their faces were very close. 'Please say yes, Donna. Say you'll marry me.'

'Yes,' she said, and her smile grew huge. 'Yes, I'll marry you.'

'Congratulations! And about time, too!' The midwife bent and plucked the sleeping infant from Donna's arms and put him gently over her shoulder. 'You and I are going down the corridor while I clean you up, young man,' she crooned softly. 'Because your father has just asked your mother to marry him, and now they want a few moments' peace and quiet to kiss each other. And they'd better make the most of it!' she finished darkly.

Donna sent a half longing glance in the direction of the door as it closed quietly behind Sister Hindmarsh and little Nick. Acknowledging already the first pangs of separation from her child. But he would be back soon.

Then she reached up her arms for Marcus, who was in the process of breaking goodness only knew how many hospital rules—since he had slipped off his canvas deck-shoes and was now sliding a delicious denim thigh forward as he joined her on the bed. He put his arms around her and looked deep into her eyes.

'When shall we get married?' he asked.

'Who cares right now?' she responded softly.

They kissed until Marcus wryly warned her that they had better stop—unless she wanted to get pregnant again! So they wrapped their arms tightly around one another instead.

And that was where Sister Hindmarsh found them when she carried their son back in—the two of them fast asleep, blissfully curled up on the hospital bed!

The baby gave a cry, and two sets of startled eyes snapped open.

'Your turn,' mumbled Donna sleepily.

'My pleasure,' murmured Marcus. He got off the bed carefully, so as not to disturb Donna, and then tenderly took his son from the midwife's arms and began to rock him.

*Harlequin truly does
make any time special....
This year we are celebrating
weddings in style!*

A
Walk
Down
the Aisle

WEDDING CELEBRATION

To help us celebrate, we want you to tell us how wearing the Harlequin wedding gown will make your wedding day special. As the grand prize, Harlequin will offer one lucky bride the chance to **"Walk Down the Aisle" in the Harlequin wedding gown!**

There's more...

For her honeymoon, she and her groom will spend five nights at the **Hyatt Regency Maui.** As part of this five-night honeymoon at the hotel renowned for its romantic attractions, the couple will enjoy a candlelit dinner for two in Swan Court, a sunset sail on the hotel's catamaran, and duet spa treatments.

A HYATT RESORT AND SPA Maui • Molokai • Lanai

To enter, please write, in, 250 words or less, how wearing the Harlequin wedding gown will make your wedding day special. The entry will be judged based on its emotionally compelling nature, its originality and creativity, and its sincerity. This contest is open to Canadian and U.S. residents only and to those who are 18 years of age and older. There is no purchase necessary to enter. Void where prohibited. See further contest rules attached. Please send your entry to:

Walk Down the Aisle Contest

In Canada	In U.S.A.
P.O. Box 637	P.O. Box 9076
Fort Erie, Ontario	3010 Walden Ave.
L2A 5X3	Buffalo, NY 14269-9076

You can also enter by visiting www.eHarlequin.com
Win the Harlequin wedding gown and the vacation of a lifetime!
The deadline for entries is October 1, 2001.

HARLEQUIN®
Makes any time special ®

PHWDACONT1

HARLEQUIN WALK DOWN THE AISLE TO MAUI CONTEST 1197
OFFICIAL RULES
NO PURCHASE NECESSARY TO ENTER

1. To enter, follow directions published in the offer to which you are responding. Contest begins April 2, 2001, and ends on October 1, 2001. Method of entry may vary. Mailed entries must be postmarked by October 1, 2001, and received by October 8, 2001.

2. Contest entry may be, at times, presented via the Internet, but will be restricted solely to residents of certain geographic areas that are disclosed on the Web site. To enter via the Internet, if permissible, access the Harlequin Web site (www.eHarlequin.com) and follow the directions displayed online. Online entries must be received by 11:59 p.m. E.S.T. on October 1, 2001.

   In lieu of submitting an entry online, enter by mail by hand-printing (or typing) on an 8½" x 11" plain piece of paper, your name, address (including zip code), Contest number/name and in 250 words or fewer, why winning a Harlequin wedding dress would make your wedding day special. Mail via first-class mail to: Harlequin Walk Down the Aisle Contest 1197, (in the U.S.) P.O. Box 9076, 3010 Walden Avenue, Buffalo, NY 14269-9076, (in Canada) P.O. Box 637, Fort Erie, Ontario L2A 5X3, Canada.

   Limit one entry per person, household address and e-mail address. Online and/or mailed entries received from persons residing in geographic areas in which Internet entry is not permissible will be disqualified.

3. Contests will be judged by a panel of members of the Harlequin editorial, marketing and public relations staff based on the following criteria:

   - Originality and Creativity—50%
   - Emotionally Compelling—25%
   - Sincerity—25%

   In the event of a tie, duplicate prizes will be awarded. Decisions of the judges are final.

4. All entries become the property of Torstar Corp. and will not be returned. No responsibility is assumed for lost, late, illegible, incomplete, inaccurate, nondelivered or misdirected mail or misdirected e-mail, for technical, hardware or software failures of any kind, lost or unavailable network connections, or failed, incomplete, garbled or delayed computer transmission or any human error which may occur in the receipt or processing of the entries in this Contest.

5. Contest open only to residents of the U.S. (except Puerto Rico) and Canada, who are 18 years of age or older, and is void wherever prohibited by law; all applicable laws and regulations apply. Any litigation within the Province of Quebec respecting the conduct or organization of a publicity contest may be submitted to the Régie des alcools, des courses et des jeux for a ruling. Any litigation respecting the awarding of a prize may be submitted to the Régie des alcools, des courses et des jeux only for the purpose of helping the parties reach a settlement. Employees and immediate family members of Torstar Corp. and D. L. Blair, Inc., their affiliates, subsidiaries and all other agencies, entities and persons connected with the use, marketing or conduct of this Contest are not eligible to enter. Taxes on prizes are the sole responsibility of winners. Acceptance of any prize offered constitutes permission to use winner's name, photograph or other likeness for the purposes of advertising, trade and promotion on behalf of Torstar Corp., its affiliates and subsidiaries without further compensation to the winner, unless prohibited by law.

6. Winners will be determined no later than November 15, 2001, and will be notified by mail. Winners will be required to sign and return an Affidavit of Eligibility form within 15 days after winner notification. Noncompliance within that time period may result in disqualification and an alternative winner may be selected. Winners of trip must execute a Release of Liability prior to ticketing and must possess required travel documents (e.g. passport, photo ID) where applicable. Trip must be completed by November 2002. No substitution of prize permitted by winner. Torstar Corp. and D. L. Blair, Inc., their parents, affiliates, and subsidiaries are not responsible for errors in printing or electronic presentation of Contest, entries and/or game pieces. In the event of printing or other errors which may result in unintended prize values or duplication of prizes, all affected game pieces or entries shall be null and void. If for any reason the Internet portion of the Contest is not capable of running as planned, including infection by computer virus, bugs, tampering, unauthorized intervention, fraud, technical failures, or any other causes beyond the control of Torstar Corp. which corrupt or affect the administration, secrecy, fairness, integrity or proper conduct of the Contest, Torstar Corp. reserves the right, at its sole discretion, to disqualify any individual who tampers with the entry process and to cancel, terminate, modify or suspend the Contest or the Internet portion thereof. In the event of a dispute regarding an online entry, the entry will be deemed submitted by the authorized holder of the e-mail account submitted at the time of entry. Authorized account holder is defined as the natural person who is assigned to an e-mail address by an Internet access provider, online service provider or other organization that is responsible for arranging e-mail address for the domain associated with the submitted e-mail address. **Purchase or acceptance of a product offer does not improve your chances of winning.**

7. Prizes: (1) Grand Prize—A Harlequin wedding dress (approximate retail value: $3,500) and a 5-night/6-day honeymoon trip to Maui, HI, including round-trip air transportation provided by Maui Visitors Bureau from Los Angeles International Airport (winner is responsible for transportation to and from Los Angeles International Airport) and a Harlequin Romance Package, including hotel accomodations (double occupancy) at the Hyatt Regency Maui Resort and Spa, dinner for (2) two at Swan Court, a sunset sail on Kiele V and a spa treatment for the winner (approximate retail value: $4,000); (5) Five runner-up prizes of a $1000 gift certificate to selected retail outlets to be determined by Sponsor (retail value $1000 ea.). Prizes consist of only those items listed as part of the prize. Limit one prize per person. All prizes are valued in U.S. currency.

8. For a list of winners (available after December 17, 2001) send a self-addressed, stamped envelope to: Harlequin Walk Down the Aisle Contest 1197 Winners, P.O. Box 4200 Blair, NE 68009-4200 or you may access the www.eHarlequin.com Web site through January 15, 2002.

Contest sponsored by Torstar Corp., P.O. Box 9042, Buffalo, NY 14269-9042, U.S.A.

PHWDACONT2

Brimming with passion and sensuality, this collection offers two full-length Harlequin Temptation novels.

Full Bloom

by *New York Times* bestselling author

JAYNE
ANN
KRENTZ

Emily Ravenscroft has had enough! It's time she took her life back, out of the hands of her domineering family and Jacob Stone, the troubleshooter they've always employed to get her out of hot water. The new Emily—vibrant and willful—doesn't need Jacob to rescue her. She needs him to love her, against all odds.

And

Compromising Positions

a brand-new story from bestselling author

VICKY LEWIS
THOMPSON

Look for it on sale September 2001.

Coming Next Month

HARLEQUIN *Presents*

THE BEST HAS JUST GOTTEN BETTER!

#2199 DUARTE'S CHILD Lynne Graham
Only days before she gave birth, Emily left her husband,
Duarte de Monteiro. Now Duarte has traced her and his baby
son, and brought them back to Portugal—because he loves her,
or just because he wants his son?

#2200 TO MAKE A MARRIAGE Carole Mortimer
Andie is convinced her baby's father is in love with another
woman. But Adam Monroe is also a close family friend—Andie
knows she can't avoid him forever....

#2201 MISTRESS BY CONTRACT Helen Bianchin
There was only one way for Mikayla to clear her father's debt to
tycoon Rafael Velez-Aguilera: offer herself in exchange! Rafael
was intrigued by Mikayla's proposal, and immediately specified
her duties as his mistress for a year!

#2202 THE ALVARES BRIDE Sandra Marton
No one knew the father of Carin's baby—but during the birth
she called out a name: Raphael Alvares! The powerful Brazilian
millionaire rushed to Carin's bedside—but had he come because
the one passionate night they'd shared had left him longing to
make Carin his bride?

#2203 LORENZO'S REWARD Catherine George
When Lorenzo Forli proposed, Jess had no qualms about letting
her husband-to-be make passionate love to her. But Lorenzo had
failed to tell Jess something about his past. Could it be that he'd
used all the means he possessed only to seduce her into his bed?

#2204 TERMS OF ENGAGEMENT Kathryn Ross
In order to avoid her ex-husband, Emma had introduced
Frazer McClarren as her new fiancé. Time and time again they
were forced to play the happy couple, but Emma could not
truly get involved with Frazer—she could never give him what
he wanted....

HPCNM0801